1

LOVING A CHAOTIC SAVAGE

(A Gangsta Love Story)

By: Author Barbie Amor
Formally known as Barbie Scott

LOVING A CHAOTIC SAVAGE

PLAYLIST – ❤☐☐☐

☐

☐

https://youtube.com/playlist?list=PLKE5pkof98ve--vRCbpm5uiA4WZBBM9DW

U Get On My Nerves- Jazmine Sullivan
Don't Let Them- Ashanti
Hey Daddy (Daddy's Home)- Usher
Party- Beyoncé
When I Get Free- Tupac
Down Ass Chick- Ja Rule
Wifey- Next
What's Love- Major Nine
Foolish-Ashanti
What These Bitches Want-DMX
Don't Mess With My Man- Nivea
Letter To Nipsey- Meek Mill
So Gone- Monica
1 Up Top Finna Drop- Mozzy
So Over You- Ashanti
U Ain't Going Nowhere- Young Buck
Marvins Room- Drake
You Belong To Somebody Else- Jacquees
Next Lifetime- Erykah Badu
When I See You- Fantasia
If You Were Mine- Nipsey Hussle
Seven Whole Days- Toni Braxton
Playa Cardz Right- Keyshia Cole
It's Whatever- Aaliyah
Just Like Daddy- Tupac

VooDoo- Ashanti
Aston Martin Music- Rick Ross
If You Love Me- Brownstone
Colors- Tee Grizzley
Big Talk- NBA YoungBoy
Buy A Heart- Nicki Minaj
Pills And Potion- Nicki Minaj
Right By My Side- Nicki Minaj ft. Chris Brown
Gangsta- Kehlani

"Desire becomes surrender and surrender becomes power!"

-The Joker

Prologue

"Amor! You guys don't go too far up the street where no one can see you."

"Okay, Mama."

"Come on, Amor, faster damn. You pushing too slow!"

"Mama said we can't go far."

"We not. We just going to the corner and turning around."

"Okay."

Karter threw his arms in the air and began to scream louder. I pushed him so fast in the metal shopping cart that my mother had stolen from Food 4 Less; my adrenaline was pumping along with his. This was something we did every day because we were too damn big to play with toys. Karter and I lived our best lives outside in our neighborhood where everyone hung out. Our neighborhood stayed lit with all the local thugs and drug dealers. Speaking of, I stopped the basket so hard Karter went crashing into the cage.

"Ouch, dumb ass!" He held the top of his head cursing me out until he realized why I had stopped. He jumped from the basket and ran over to Pack before I got to him.

"Pack, let me get five dollars." Karter smiled widely.

Without any words, Pack rushed into his pocket and pulled out a wad of money. He handed the bill to Karter, then looked at me. "Here, Amor," Pack called out to me.

I ran over to him and quickly took the five-dollar-bill from his hand.

"Thank you." I smiled shyly, then ran back over to Karter.

"Let's go to the store?" Karter wasted no time asking.

"We gotta go tell Mommy first, foo."

"Aye, Pack, if Mama comes looking for us, tell her we at the store!" Karter told Pack, smiling.

"A'ight, little nigga. Y'all hurry back."

"Let's go, bald headed girl." Karter slapped me in the back of my head.

"I'mma beat yo' ass," I told him as I shoved my money into my pocket.

"You gotta catch me first, bald head!"

He broke wind on me with a goofy grin. He then ran at full speed toward the liquor store, and by the time I caught up with him, he was running inside. He ducked down behind one of the aisles, so I outsmarted him. I headed to the back of the store and looked into the huge circle mirror above. Karter was trying so hard to creep he didn't know I was watching him. I ran down the fourth aisle because I knew he was coming toward me, and as soon as he hit the corner, he bumped right into me and began screaming with laughter. I had scared his butt, and it was so funny that I couldn't beat his ass like I had intended. We both laughed and began running around the store making sure to spend the whole five dollars. By the time we were done, we had chips, pop, candy, and I had even stole a couple of other things.

Once we were done, we walked out the store with our black plastic bags in our hands. Karter tore into his chips while I ate my Now & Laters one by one. We both were silent until Karter brought me from my thoughts.

"Man, I can't wait to get older and get some money," he said in a rushed tone.

"And how do you plan on getting money?"

"NFL," he boasted.

"You weak, Karter."

"Girl, I'mma beast. Just watch, bald head, when you ask for a *house."*

"Call me bald-headed again." I stopped him, ready to play fight.

He began laughing like he always did, with his goofy self. "You are bald-headed, though, Amor." His two big front teeth clowned and took off running.

"Yeah, well, yo' teeth look like two chicklets, and your head is..." I went to speak as I got ready to run after him.

Before I could get a good pace, gunshots began echoing through the air. My first instinct was to hit the ground. I hit it so hard my head went crashing into the cement. My eyes wandered up the street, and the neighborhood guys were a few feet away from us. I saw two bodies hit the ground, but I couldn't tell if they were shot. The sound of more gunshots rang out, and that was when it hit me, Karter! I began looking around for him. I noticed his body hanging off the sidewalk while his head was pressed into the passenger tire of an old worn down minivan.

"Karter!" I called his name, so he could get up. When he didn't move, I stood to my feet and walked over to him. In the distance, I could hear my mother screaming my name, but I had to get Karter. "Karter." I called his name just above a whisper, and again, he didn't move. I bent down and snatched him up, and that was when I noticed blood seeping from his head. I began to panic, but it was like my voice was caught in my throat. I fell to the ground with Karter wrapped in my arms, and when I realized my little brother wasn't getting up, I began screaming as I rocked his body back and forth. "Karter! Please!"

CHAPTER ONE

Amor

I swear that I don't know how we lasted that long,
You get on my damn nerves- Jazmine Sullivan

12 Years Later....

Hearing the sound of a phone vibrating through the floor broke me from my sleep, so I lifted from my bed and picked up Ruger's pants. I knew it wasn't my phone because I had that same annoying iPhone ringtone everyone else had; unless you were important, and I stored you under a song. As I began to go through his pockets, I kept my eye on him as he slept peacefully from the good loving I had just put on him. I fumbled with his pants until I pulled out a black cell phone that I had never seen. When I flipped the phone open, the caller had hung up, but that didn't stop me from searching further. First, I went to the contacts, but not one number was stored. Therefore, I went to the texts and began to read.

Sunday 4:32 p.m.
Me: *Man I love you, and whatever I could do to get you back, I'll try.*

(323) 671-0018: *You got a bitch, so just leave me alone.*

Me: *Man, this shit ain't the same. I still love you.*

(323) 671-0018: *Whatever, Ruger. Prove it.*

Me: *A'ight, don't trip.*

Tuesday 8:13 a.m.

Me: *Good Morning.*

(323) 671-0018: *Morning.*

Me: *Can I take you to breakfast?*

(323) 671-0018: *Yes. When you coming?*

Tuesday 11:22 a.m.

Me: *Aye, I'm outside.*

As I read the texts between Ruger and the unknown number, it didn't take a rocket scientist to realize it was his ex, who he was with right before me. Tears poured down my face as my eyes scanned each thread. This was the third time I had found a text from a bitch. First, it was a bitch he met at the club, and before that, it was a bitch who lived in the hood. Now, here it was, the bitch who'd left him for dead in jail and started a relationship with his enemy, was now back in our lives, ready to corrupt our relationship.

Not being able to contain myself any longer, I ran over to Ruger's bedside and hit his ass with his phone so hard he woke up out of his sleep holding his head. He looked around the room not knowing what happened until he studied my expression, then his eyes darted down to the phone.

"On, Piru, you got me fucked up!" I banged on his ass ready to go blow for blow. I never used my hood shit loosely; unless I was mad, and right now, this nigga had me all the way fucked up. I swear he was gonna keep testing me until I put a bullet through his fucking heart. Ru knew my gangsta, but he constantly tested me. "So you still in love with yo' ex bitch, huh?" I fumed as I eagerly slid into my pants. I didn't give a fuck that this was my home; he could have this shit for all I cared. "I swear you ain't shit. You swear you so different, but you just like the rest of these niggas," I continued to badger him.

Because of his guilt, he remained quiet, and the shit pissed me off more. He had this dumb ass look on his face that irritated the fuck outta me. His long locs hung over his hooded eyes, but I could still read the regret of being caught slipping. This nigga ain't regret hurting me; he regretted getting caught. Ru didn't love me, or at least that was how I felt. There wasn't any love or affection in our home.

No slaps on the ass when I walked by.

No kisses on the neck while I cleaned the house.

Definitely no romance.

I just didn't understand it for the life of me. I mean, I knew I wasn't the baddest bitch on earth, but I was cute. I stood at five-seven with a golden brown complexion. I had what some-one would refer to as doe-shaped eyes, and the curve in my top lip made niggas melt. I was thick as fuck with the right curves, and because of my height, I ain't look fat. My hair grade was good because my grandmother was full-blooded Hispanic, so it hung long down my back. Therefore, I never understood why he acted like I wasn't shit.

The bitches he chased made me look like a complete fool. Them dusty bitches couldn't fuck with me on my worst day be-cause I made sure to stay fly. Not only that, but I played my part around the house. I lit candles and wore the sexiest outfits I could find in the drawer. Shit, had it been any other nigga, I would have kept their dick at attention. But, nah, Ru? He acted like I didn't exist. If he wasn't in the hood with the homies, he was on his video game ignoring the fuck out of me. I'd bust my ass around the house cooking, cleaning, and working my job as a tax auditor. Don't ask me how I got the job because I didn't know. My record was fucked up, I had tattoos on my face, and it was evident I was a hood chick. However, when I spoke, not only pro-fessionally, but in Spanish, they hired my ass on the spot.

Once I was done putting on my shoes, I jumped up and grabbed my purse and keys. When I heard the creaking from the bed, I knew he was getting up, so I sprinted for the door and slammed it shut behind me. I climbed into my car, and before he could make it to the door, I pulled out of the yard and headed for the studio. The studio was where I went when I needed to relieve some stress. Although I didn't take my rap career as serious as I should have, it was still an adrenaline rush for me. I always put my emotions into my lyrics, and it helped me escape those dark places I frequently visited.

Ever since my little brother was murdered, I fell into a depression and began rapping. My peers always told me I should take my career more seriously, but I just wasn't feeling it. I had a few music videos and even performed a few times, but over time, I had lost the passion. Being a tax auditor wasn't my dream job, but it paid the bills.

I tried hard not to go back to the old me, which consisted of hugging the block with a sack of dope. Other than music and my job, I was a typical hood chick with dreams of leaving the hood. This wasn't my life, but being a product of my environment, I was sucked in. My little brother's death wasn't an excuse, but then again, it was. I knew everyone in my hood, and they watched me grow up, however, like I said, I had no intentions of gang-banging. After Karter was killed, and I found out who was responsible for his death, I started gang-banging heavily and going after anybody held accountable. I never found out who actually pulled the trigger, but when I heard it was our rival enemies, it was on. I suited up with Ru, and went through there every chance I had gotten. My little brother was my life, and after his death, my mom moved out of state. That was another thing that made me depressed. My mom was all I had, and now, I was stuck here with Ru's cheating ass.

The sound of my phone ringing made me look over toward my purse. It was going on three a.m., so I knew it could only be three people. Ruger, who I wasn't fucking with right now, or my homegirls, Rawdy and Misha. Knowing Ruger, he probably called Misha because he knew she was the only one who could talk some sense into me. When I picked up the phone, I dropped it the minute I saw Ruger's number. I let his ass go to voicemail, and he called back nonstop. I swear I was so tired of this nigga it wasn't funny. I had been preaching these same words for two years, and the shit was beginning to play out. I was trying to give this nigga the benefit of the doubt and prayed one day he'd realize who really held him down, but he ain't take heed.

Ruger and I had known each other all our lives, but we had only been officially together for two years. It was one of those "late nights in the hood, and a bitch was vulnerable, so we fucked" type of moments. I had just broken up with a nigga named Clyde, but that was another story for another day. Just know the relationship with Clyde was a bit complex, but we ended it on good terms. I really didn't mean for a relationship to come out of Ru, and because I knew the type of nigga he was, I was supposed to fuck and keep it pushing. My bad for slipping up.

At the time, he was fresh out of a relationship when we got together, so we were both in similar situations. However, he was still in love with the bitch and playing mind games with me. At one point, I really loved Ru because the thrill of having a nigga hug the block with me was always so dope to me. Who better to have my back than a nigga from the same hood? Our hood bonded us together, but I guess it wasn't enough to intertwine our hearts.

"'Sup, Amor?"

I nodded my head and took a seat on the empty sofa near the small fridge. I could feel Lex's eyes watching me, but I busied myself with my phone.

"Amor, you recording tonight, ma?" Lex asked.

"No, not tonight." I faintly smiled with a heavy heart.

I could feel Lex's eyes burning a massive hole throughout my body.

"Let me guess. That nigga Ruger?" He shook his head already knowing why I was here.

When it came to Moe, Fab, and Lex, these niggas saw right threw me. These were my boys. They consoled me on many of my bitter nights, and they knew the full details about my relationship with Ru. Hell, I put all my emotions into my music, and they were no fools. What I liked about these niggas was, none of them tried to sleep with me, and it was strictly business. Well, except for Lex, who was in love with me, but when I turned him down, he never pressed me. They weren't from the hood, so anytime I was around them, I could relax with no gang ties.

Nodding my head *yes*, I couldn't lie if I wanted to. I was so embarrassed I broke eye contact with Lex and dropped my head back into my phone.

"Stop settling, girl. I keep telling yo' ass." Fab shook his head again and focused back on his work.

"You ready to shoot the 'Certified' video?" Lex asked with his face tight.

I knew he felt just as Fab did because he couldn't stand Ru. He never really got into our business, and I also knew a part of that hate came from the relationship I had with Ru. Truth be told, Lex was madly in love with me. Lex had a girlfriend who he was on the verge of breaking up with, and I just couldn't be a nigga's rebound. Not only that, but I was a virgin at the time, so he tried hard to slide his way in. These niggas thought because I was as hood as they come, I was loose like girls around my way. However, that wasn't the case. Not too many people knew I was a virgin at the time, and I held my sacred tunnel as long as I could. I gave my virginity to Clyde, fucked with a few niggas after, then I slipped up with Ru.

"I'm ready," I replied to Lex with confidence. It was time we shot a video for my track called 'Certified.'

A part of me was excited because I hadn't shot in a minute, and I needed this so my following could rise. I had a decent following due to my music and my tax work, but I needed more so I could make revenue. Once I got to 100K, I was gonna start an online boutique and target the divas who fucked with me.

"A'ight, we gonna shoot on the twenty-seventh. You got a couple weeks to get yourself together. I'll hit Stacy for wardrobe."

"Okay," I replied sadly because my mind drifted to Ru.

It was taking everything in me not to cry right now because the thought of shooting this video without him was hurtful. Ru was at all my events and shoots. And right now, my mind was telling me I was done, but my heart spoke differently. Who was I kidding? I loved this nigga.

CHAPTER TWO

Amor

"Say that you want me
Say that you'll never leave me
You gotta tell me you need me"
Don't let them take your love away

-Ashanti

Two weeks Later...

"You okay, Amor?"
"Yes, I'm fine. It must've been something I ate."

"Either that, or that bun in the oven."

"I'm fine, Misha."

I stood to my feet and retrieved the glass of water she was holding. She had her brow raised and her weight shifted to one side. She wore a look as if she wasn't buying what I was selling, which was dumb because if I *was* pregnant, she would be the first to know. Mish was not only my homegirl from my hood but also my best friend. Rawdy was another one of my best friends, but she was so damn hood it interfered in our friendship. All she did was hang out, shoot dice, and sell dope while Mish and I worked. Mish worked at Shiekh Shoes inside the mall. She had been there three years now and was attending school. Rawdy, on the other hand, bled the block day in and day out, and that was all her life consisted of. Now, don't get me wrong, I bled the block and dabbled in a little drug selling, but the shit wasn't for me no more. I wanted more for myself, so I left the street hustling up to Ru.

"Well, Lex is ready for you on set. Get it together." She began fluffing a few of my curls.

I gave myself a double-check in the mirror, then bent down to rinse my mouth. Once I was done, I left the dressing room and headed outside.

The moment I stepped out the door, Ru was standing over by the lowrider Lex had rented for the shoot. He and I locked eyes, and for a split second, I fell into a repentant daze. I was so ashamed by Ru's presence because all eyes were on me. Everyone around us stood motionless by him being here, and I knew what they were thinking: I was stupid.

After the night I left the studio, I headed home because Misha wasn't answering, and Rawdy was out with her boo. I stayed at the studio until the wee hours of the morning hoping he would leave and go to his grandmother's. However, that didn't happen. He stayed at my house and waited for me by the door. ☐ When I walked in, he had tears in his eyes and pleaded for my forgiveness. Of course, my stupid ass fell for the okie doke. We ended up making love, and now, look. A bitch was running to the restroom throwing up her guts.

I was no fool. As much as I didn't want to admit it, I was pregnant. Yet, I was gonna continue to be in denial, and until I took a test, I wouldn't accept it. I had a period last month, but that ain't mean shit. I knew my body, and it wasn't the meatloaf I ate earlier.

"Not now, we got work," Lex said, pulling my attention from Ru.

Ruger watched us with easy eyes but continued leaning on the lowrider in a cool state. He wore a white shirt with a bandana around the collar and pocket just as I wore for one scene. I assumed he was gonna hop in a few shots, and that was tricky because Lex didn't even want him here.

By the time we were done with the shoot, I was tired as hell and too tired to go out. Ru and I were supposed to go to dinner, but the way my tummy was set up, I just wanted to curl up with a lemon. As we headed for my crib, we made small talk, but things were still shaky. I wanted so bad to bring up the situation about me possibly being pregnant; I just didn't know how. A part of me felt like he'd be disappointed in me, but he didn't have to worry because I was getting rid of it regardless.

"Ru, I...I have something I wanna tell you." I stumbled over my words as I bit into my bottom lip. I watched the side structure of his face, and his sexy, chiseled chin got tight.

He looked over at me, and I could tell he was skeptical

about what would come out of my mouth. "I'm listening," he replied, facing the road.

"I think I'm pregnant, but it's nothing you have to worry about. I'm gonna make an appointment for an abortion in the morning if I am."

"Damn, so you just ain't gon' give me a say so? Fuck how I feel?"

"It's not like that. I just thought that—"

"You thought *shit*, Amor. You having my baby, and that's that."

I rolled my eyes and popped the fuck out of my neck in his direction. "I'm not 'bout to bring no baby into this tainted-ass relationship. You want me to have yo' baby, then you gotta get yo' shit together. And anyway, I don't have time for a baby. I'm trying to live my dreams."

"And what's that? 'Cause yo' ass don't take your music serious. Cut the shit, shorty. You knew what could happen, and you chose not to get no birth control. If you is pregnant, I want my baby, so you can have it and give it to me," he replied just as he parked in the driveway.

Without another word, I climbed out of the car and headed for the door. This conversation was far from over, so I quickly moved to unlock the door. I headed straight for my bedroom and ran my shower. Ru took a seat on the bed and began taking his shoes off. I peeled out of my clothing, and before I could walk into the restroom, he grabbed me roughly and sat my body on the dresser. I knew what this meant. He was about to give me his Grammy award-winning head job that was gonna have a bitch catching convulsions.

Just the thought alone made me anxiously spread my legs and invite him in. Without warning, he dropped to his knees and wrapped the cuffs of my legs into the fold of his arms and came face to face with my love box. He knew what I liked, he knew exactly how I liked it, so he wasted no time taking me to my peak. He clutched his mouth around my clitoris and began to tease it with his tongue. In an instant, I began to moan as I grabbed into his locks and pushed him further inside.

"Ohhh, shit, Ru," I called out as the back of my head touched the glass attached to our dresser. I continued to push his head into my opening while he went to work.

Suddenly, he stopped and looked up at me. "You gon' have my baby?" he asked compellingly.

I looked him in the eyes, and I couldn't deny this nigga if I wanted to. I loved Ru despite the bullshit he took me through. There weren't always bitter moments. Some were actually sweet and loving. The nigga would jump in front of me at the sound of a gunshot.

"Yes," I replied, unmoved, but slightly confused.

"I love you, Amor. I'll do anything for you, ma. These otha' hoes don't mean shit to me," he spoke with persuasion.

I wanted so badly to believe him, but his track record was fucked up. Instead of replying, I kissed his lips and slid my body down, so he could give me some dick. Right now, I didn't have much to say because I wasn't trying to become vulnerable to his lies. I wanted his dick with no conversation about the baby. I didn't know for sure if I was pregnant, so I wasn't gonna jump the gun.

The next morning, I was off work, so I was up and dressed to hang on the block with my homies. Ru and I left our home and headed for the hood but made sure we stopped and grabbed some breakfast first. When we pulled up, everybody was on the block. We found a park right in front of Rawdy's crib and walked the short block up the street.

Misha was off to work, and she was getting off at three. Rawdy was outside, of course, because she was chasing the new little bitch who moved in the hood. That was something I failed to mention. Rawdy was a stud but cute and rough. She had that Young MA look and stayed fresh to death. Her face had a few tattoos, along with her body that was flooded with ink.

"Yo ass betta' had brought me something." Rawdy reached for my bag of food.

Ru walked over to talk to the homie, Boss, so Rawdy and I began to clown. It was gonna be a typical day in the hood. By nightfall, we'd end up with a few bottles and crowds of people from all over.

CHAPTER THREE

Chaotic

"Is you say Daddy's home, home for me
And I know you've been waiting for this love in your day..."
-Usher

S tepping from behind the walls after six long years, I felt like that nigga despite the circumstances. I was finally free, and the world wasn't ready for a cocky nigga like me. I knew many would think that time did something to me, and y'all right, it did. It didn't take the savage out of me, but it made me a lot wiser for these cold pavements I was about to endure. After watching niggas die in front of my eyes and getting it out the mud while behind bars, a nigga was ready for society. I spent too many of my days surrounded by pussy ass COs and the fake "high power" niggas on a yard. I was ready to get back to the money and fuck the shit out of Ashley, who was currently my bitch. I needed some pussy bad, and I had a boat-load of skeet to release on somebody's face.

I stepped out of the huge black fence that closed behind me, and Ashley was waiting right there with a huge grin on her face. Lil' mama didn't even know what was in store for her. She wore a short ass skirt with a shirt that was too damn little for them big ass titties, but she looked good. The smile that was plastered on her face made me feel good that she was excited to see me, and it made me more content with the relationship.

I wasn't the type of nigga to love a bitch, but after six years of holding me down, I felt indebted. I never expected no bitch to do any time with me because I knew how this shit was: out of sight, out of mind. But Ashley played her part, so in return, I was gonna try.

"Baaaae." She smiled and wrapped her arms around me as soon as I was in arm's reach.

"You missed me?" I asked, pulling her in for a hug.

"Of course, I missed you," she replied, and my dick stood at attention. "You ain't ready." She laughed and playfully hit me in the chest.

"Shidddd?" I laughed back, making my way to her whip.

I was ready to get the fuck from right here. She followed my lead toward the driver's seat and climbed in. We pulled off and headed for the airport. Because I had to be at the Halfway House by three p.m., I only had a few hours to spend with her. On our way to the airport, we made small talk, and she filled me in on things going on in the streets. By the time we made it, she had given me an earful. It was only seven a.m., and our flight was due to land at 10:42 a.m.

After we boarded the plane, I got good and comfortable and trained my attention out the window. I was finally free. Other than getting some pussy, I was ready to take the world by surprise. Many days, I thought of opening a few trap houses, so I wouldn't go back to robbing. That was my goal, and when I wanted something, I made sure to get it.

Ashley took my hand into hers and squeezed it. I felt awkward as hell, but because I wanted to try this relationship shit, I ain't trip.

I kissed her cheek and turned back in my seat. I looked back out the window, and for the entire flight, I studied the clouds in a trance.

❤️□□□

When we made it to Ashley's crib, that was now my new home, it wasn't really what I expected, but, shit, it was home. We headed inside, and I went straight for the shower. To my surprise, she gave me some space, and the entire time I soaped up, my dick was hard. Because I knew I was gonna nut fast, I cheated by jacking off. When I was done, I stepped out and headed into the bedroom wrapped in a towel.

Ashley was lying on the bed naked, and the hunger in her eyes told me she was ready for this dick. Because she wasn't my bitch when I first went, and in the feds, we didn't have cell phones, she never got a chance to see my dick. Therefore, I pulled the towel off, and her eyes shot open wide. I smirked on the low because all that shit she was talking she wasn't backing up. Although I was a cocky ass nigga, I wasn't one to brag. My dick was eleven inches long, and I knew this because I measured it myself before. □

"You a big girl, right?"

"Ye...hmm.." she cleared her throat. "Yeah, nigga," she replied with fake confidence.

I laughed and climbed in the bed. Because of her frightened look, I spared baby girl and let her lie down. I hiked her leg up and slid the tip in from the side. She let out a soft gasp, and when I felt her body relax, I slid the rest of my ten inches inside of her. I was gonna punish this poor girl, but I started off slow to get her used to me. As I began stroking her, I couldn't see her facial expressions, but the way she was screaming made my dick harder.

"Canyon, baby! You're hurting me!" she tried to run, but I grabbed her around her waist.

"Where you going?"

"You hurting me, babe."

"A'ight."

I slowed down, and her screams turned into moans. I wasn't the type of nigga to make love, so she was gonna have to get control of herself. This relationship shit was new to me, but because of my previous girlfriend, before I went, it helped me understand a few things. It helped me realize I could sit my ass down. It also helped me understand women more and with the help of a book called *Adam and Eve Syndrome* I read in prison, I knew everything about a bitch.

Nicole was the bitch I had when I went to prison, and that only lasted six months. Baby girl kept shit real and told me she couldn't do jail, and just like that, she was gone. Another thing I learned from that relationship was to always follow a woman's intuition. The night, I was heading out the door to hit this casino lick. Nicole looked me in the eyes and told me not to go. Instead of listening, I went, and my ass went straight to jail. Lesson learned. This was the reason I couldn't be mad she left. However, I did expect her to make sure a nigga was straight. That bitch left a nigga high and dry with not even as much as a letter.

"Ohhhh, shit, I'm 'bout to cummm. Canyon, I'm cumming..."

"Let that shit out."

I took that as my opportunity to stroke her harder. Shortly

after, I followed behind her, and I could feel my nut ooze inside of her. When I rolled off her, she lay flat on her stomach, and I could tell she was done. I wasn't done with her ass, but because I ain't have much time left, I spared her.

It was now going on 1:48 p.m., and it would take us an hour to get to the facility. I climbed out the bed and headed into the restroom for another shower. I quickly washed off and jumped out to slide into my clothes. Before walking out the door, I looked around the house trying to adjust to my surroundings.

"I'mma miss you." Ashley appeared from the bedroom and leaned against the doorway.

"I'll be back." I hit her with a smile and was out the door.

When I hit the pavement, I looked up into the sun, then let out a deep sigh. *Daddy's home.* I smiled to myself and went to face this facility and these fake police.

CHAPTER FOUR

Amor

*"You a bad girl and your friends bad too, ooh
We got the swag sauce, she drippin' swagu..."*
-Beyonce

"**G**et dressed. We heading to the club." Ru walked in dressed fresh from head to toe.

I couldn't front. He was lookin' good with his locks freshly twisted and a fresh outfit from Dior.

"What club?"

"The homie just opened a club. He wants me to come up there and watch his back."

"Dang, I can't drink or nothing," I complained because I

hated the fact I couldn't turn up.

"You don't even know if you pregnant yet, girl. Just get up. Call yo' girls."

"Okay. I'm 'bout to get up."

I picked up my phone to call Rawdy and Misha. When they both agreed to roll, I got up and began getting dressed. If I was pregnant, I wasn't big yet, so I decided to get cute. I slid on a white off-shoulder dress that hugged every curve. I chose off-white tenny shoes because I wanted to be comfortable. My hair was already slayed with a middle part hanging down my shoulders, and because I didn't wear makeup, I only had to apply gloss.

When I headed to the front, Rawdy was already in the living room with a few of the homies, and Misha had texted saying she was on her way. We all headed outside to wait for Misha, and while we waited, Rawdy rolled up a few blunts. Ru and the homies started sippin' on Hennessy, but I was gonna wait until we got there to drink. After about twenty minutes, Mish pulled up, so we headed West for the club.

When we pulled up, we all bounced out the car and headed for the gate. We were greeted by Dolla, one of the homies from the West. He and Ru were boys from doing a bid in Delano State Prison together, and he knew Ru was a businessman. Not to mention, he'd bust a gun for him, and that was really why we were here.

"Y'all go chill in VIP. I'mma go holla at Dolla and see what he wants me to do."

"Okay, and don't make me fuck you up, Ru."

"Come on, shorty, I ain't on none of that." He kissed my

cheek and walked off.

The club was packed for it to have been so early, and I knew Ru wasn't tripping off these niggas because the homies was with us.

"Pour us some drank, Misha," Rawdy told her because she was the closest to the ice bucket and cups. Rawdy then stood to her feet and headed over to the strippers.

Misha and I were already used to her ratchet antics, so we let her do her. However, she wasn't gonna go far because if it was one thing about Rawdy, she stayed strapped and would protect us with her dear life. No matter where we went, and whether I had my strap or not, she would still act like our damn guard.

❤️▢▢▢

"Yeah, that nigga, Chaotic, out."

"Word?" Lil' Ru replied to Boss, looking surprised.

They had begun to chat about this Chaotic nigga, so I took this as my chance to get up. I was good and drunk and ready to pop my ass on Ru. The entire night, he had come every so often, but he hadn't been back for over an hour.

"Where you going?" Boss stopped in the middle of his conversation to ask.

I turned around and looked at him like he was crazy.
"To find my nigga damn." I mugged his nosey ass, and he looked like he wanted to object.

He quickly jumped on his phone, so I waved his ass off and headed outside to find Ru.

When I made it outside, Ru was standing by the gate with his phone in hand.

"He ain't have to warn you by telling you I'm coming." I rolled my eyes already knowing what was going on.

"What you talkin' 'bout girl?" he asked, shoving his phone into his pocket.

"Ru, I'm not dumb. Anyway." I rolled my eyes again dismissing the bullshit they were pulling.

"Amor, take yo' ass inside."

"Why? I miss you."

"It ain't safe out here. That's why." He lifted up from the pole he was leaning on and approached the females who were walking through the gate. "Open y'all bags," Ru told the chicks, and they did as told.

I stood to the side for a moment, and when I heard Beyonce's "Party" come on inside, I left. No matter how old the song had gotten, it was my shit, and I'd always turn up.

Just as I expected, Misha had a nigga hemmed up on the wall, and Rawdy was still entertaining strippers. Same scene as before, and this was why I left in the first place. I was nice and buzzed and began to feel bored. I wanted to finish drinking, but unsure if I was pregnant or not, I chose to stop. I sat in my original seat and began scrolling through my phone. The homies were still talking 'bout this Chaotic nigga, so I couldn't help but over hear. I had heard his name in the streets, but I had never seen him. I did know he was an enemy, and by the way they were talking, I could tell he was a threat; therefore, he had to be eliminated.

CHAPTER FIVE

Chaotic

"When I get free, motherfuckers better watch they ass
Soon as I get released, I'mma clock some cash
Did some time locked down, but I'm back on the street
There'll be trouble when they see me..."
-Tupac

Aafter thirty long ass days of sitting in that whack ass half-way house, I was finally let free on my first pass. I slid to Ashley's, hit her with some dope dick, then left for my hood. I pulled up to the park where I knew niggas were hanging out and jumped out a rental car fresh as fuck. I made my way to a crowd of niggas, and when they saw it was me, everyone stopped. Some niggas were greasy by my presence, and a few were happy to see a nigga.

Like the cocky nigga I was, I bypassed the crowd and shook one nigga's hand. As I began talking to my nigga, Shorty, I noticed my lil' brother across the park. When he looked up and spotted me, I saw the wide grin appear on his face, and that made me smile hard. My little brother was my keeper. He was holding shit down in the hood while I was away, and I swear our attitudes were a spit image of each other. He had plenty enemies, a cocky ass demeanor, and chanced his life for a bag. Niggas really hated his mean ass but wouldn't dare fuck with him because they knew my capability. I would push a nigga wig over my brother and vice versa.

"Welcome home, square ass nigga." He grabbed my hand and pulled me in for a hug. "I got some bread for you." He reached into his pocket and pulled out a huge stack.

I stuffed that shit in my pocket proud my young nigga was doing his shit and still on the streets.

"Good looking."

"You holla at Mama?"

"Yeah, I touched with her. I'mma shoot over there in a minute."

"A'ight, let me know when you ready," he replied as his phone rang.

A few more niggas walked over to us, and this was what I needed. I had some shit to say, and I needed everyone's attention. "I got shit to do, so I'mma make this quick. I got this little bitch who just put three spots in her name. I need some solid niggas in 'em. Shorty gon' run the main/ second house, and little bro gon' run the third. I'mma be in the first house from time to time, and El gon' run shit when I'm not there. Now y'all know the way I get my bag, so that trap boy shit ain't my main focus. Fucking with them Feds, I gotta stay off the radar, so I won't be around much. I got the Mexicans off the ten who gon' front me ten bricks and I'mma buy ten. After I pay them niggas, its only up from there," I spoke, looking around the crowd.

The entire time, I noticed who was supposed to be my homie looking greasy perusal. He stood off to the side, and the hate in his eyes was evident. He knew my get down, and he hated the power I had. What the little nigga needed to understand was, this hood ain't make me a gangsta; I brought my gangsta to the hood. These niggas was comfortable with taking they gangsta off at night like a Pro Club t-shirt; my shit was branded in me for life.

"Tuck, you got something you wanna say?" I put him on blast.

He looked at me, and the minute our eyes locked, his facial expression changed. "Nah," he replied without making eye contact.

"I didn't think so." I mugged the nigga, but he ain't reply.

My little bro looked at me, then him, and I could see it in his eyes he was ready to go up on the nigga. However, I had bigger fish to fry. Therefore, I finished running over the plan, then told my little bro let's roll. We headed out the park for mom's crib.

When we pulled up, I noticed my BM's car, so that meant she was dropping my son off. I quickly deaded the engine and headed in eager as fuck to see my little nigga. It'd been six long years, and when I left, he was eight.

When I walked in the crib, mom was in the kitchen pulling a pan from the oven. The smell of crab legs and Old Bay lingered in the air making me hungry. My mom knew I loved seafood just as much as her. I headed over to give her a hug, and Lil' Canyon walked in coolly. He looked at me and smiled. I sized him up and noticed how much he had grown. I got pictures of him while locked up, but the pics ain't do no justice because he was much taller in person.

"What's up, Dad?" He smirked, watching me.

"Nigga, bring yo' little ass here."

He walked over to me and gave me a hug. I knew right then he was a mature young man and not the same baby boy I had left. When he was a baby, I kept his little ass by my side right in my passenger seat.

"Hey, Canyon," my BM got up from the table and spoke.

"Sup?" was all I replied because I ain't wanna give the wrong impression.

I mean, there wasn't too much to say to each other, so she headed out the door, and I continued on with my son.

After fucking with my son for a while longer, I went into the kitchen and wrapped my arms around my mother. Because she was so small, I towered over her small frame, and at this very moment, it felt good to be home. I had the people I loved most standing right here in this room. Them days away from my family was the only thing that fucked up my mental. Besides them, I did my time with ten toes to the concrete and held my head high. I ran that prison yard, and the niggas who were "somebody" were making me rice bowls. I was that nigga, and now that I was back on the streets, I was gonna shake this shit up.

After chopping it up with my son and moms, Lil' Canyon went back to his video game, so me and lil' bro headed for the living room to wait on the food. He began catching me up on shit I missed and even went to YouTube to put me up on the latest music. One video in particular came on, and the chick rapping piqued my interest. Not in a satisfying way but because she had on my enemy's colors.

"Who this lil' bitch?"

"That's Amor. She from Piru," he replied as I zoomed in on her.

I couldn't front. She was thick as fuck but from the wrong side of the fence. I was very familiar with the Pirus because my pops was from over there. Everyone expected me to be from that side, but that was out. When my pops got murdered, I was a young nigga with no understanding.

"She cool, bro," he added, and I assumed it was because of the frown on my face.

He was vouching for her, but for some reason, she had me pressured. She was in the video wearing all-burgundy and walking down the street like she was tougher than these niggas. It was a trip. I'd never heard of her because my name rang bells, and I knew everybody who was somebody.

"Man, fuck that bitch." I mugged, and my bro started laughing.

I ain't see shit funny because I meant it. I made him start the video over, and after that, we continued to the next set of videos. He lit him a blunt and waited for my moms to come hit it. Because I was on parole, I couldn't smoke, so I just sat back and watched TV.

CHAPTER SIX

Amor

"'Cause I'm your bitch, the Bonnie to your Clyde
It's mental, mash your enemies, we out in the rental
I'm your bitch, niggas run up on ya,
Shift ya lungs, who's your organ donor?"
-Charli Baltimore

Two months later

It was the night of my birthday, and a bitch couldn't stop throwing up. I still hadn't taken the test, but I knew I was pregnant for sure. I wasn't showing yet, but I had to be about three and a half months. I had an appointment tomorrow, but tonight, I was gonna turn up.

I wasn't gonna drink because Ru wasn't having it, but that didn't mean I couldn't have fun. We were dressed and ready to head to Dolla's club just as we had been doing for the last two months. His spot had become a regular, and I even brought a nice crowd. Ru was now his paid security, so he not only secured the party, but he was selling his work to everyone who took it up the nose coming in.

When we pulled up, Ru looked at me and smiled. There were red and black balloons outside, and the crowd that was here tonight were all my homies and friends.

"Happy Birthday, shorty." He reached over and kissed my cheek.

I smiled gracefully and jumped out of the car excited. Everyone began to scream, "Happy birthday!" as I made my way inside. Misha and my coworker, Jami, were the first to approach me, and instantly, we began mingling through the crowd.

"Who's that?" Jami slurred, already drunk, looking at some chick who had just walked by.

I'd seen the chick a few times and couldn't forget her if I wanted to. She had a big ghetto booty and always wore the same white jeans. She was looking in my direction, but when we all looked at her, she quickly turned her head.

"I don't know. Prolly just a fan." I waved the bitch off and turned back to look at my friends.

We began indulging in a conversation about me being pregnant, and Dolla came in screaming my name. The way he was calling me I knew something had to be wrong. I prayed like hell it wasn't Ru because we had just begun to celebrate my day. It was bad enough I couldn't drink, so I definitely didn't need no bullshit.

"Sup, everything good?"

"Man, the ones outside. They ran up on Ru, and he had that shit in his pocket."

"What?" I asked as I ran past him.

Sure enough, they had Ru at the car, and the drugs sitting on the trunk. We made eye contact, and that told me not to say shit. He knew I was about to go the fuck off because he knew how I felt about the police. Because I was on a seven-year joint suspension for a gun case, I only watched. When they put him in the car, Misha and me jumped into hers, and she drove me home. I wasn't gonna wait until he called because I wasn't a waiting type of bitch. I was gonna go straight to my stash, then straight for the bail bond.

❤️□□□

Five hours later, they had finally given Ru a bail, and he was being released. It was now going on four in the morning, and I was dog ass tired. I sat outside the jail waiting on him to be released, and I wasn't leaving until he was out. I was in and out of sleep until I saw his tall frame coming through the glass doors. I jumped out of the car and ran over to him and hugged him tight.

"Let's go home, baby." He pulled me toward the car, and we climbed in. "What time yo' appointment?"

"Nine."

"A'ight, well, get you some rest when we get home."

"Okay." I lay my head back. "So you 'bout to have a case?" I asked because I knew how this shit was gonna go. Court date after court date, then he'd have to get probation. Because it'd been years since his last case, he wasn't on any parole or probation, so, definitely, he would come off with a slap on the wrist.

"Yeah and no. I might can get off on a proposition thirty-six. Do some drug classes and shit." His phone began ringing, but he never bothered to answer. He kept his head straight, and I could tell a lot was on his mind.

When Ru went silent on me, I began dozing off until

we pulled up at home. I headed straight for the shower, then climbed into my bed to sleep for a couple hours.

"I'm 'bout to go to the hood for a minute." Ru walked in and kissed my cheek.

I nodded my head, half asleep, as his frame disappeared out the door.

"Amor, get up, ma."

I heard Ru's voice as I stirred in my sleep. When I opened my eyes, I was dog ass tired, and it felt like I had just closed my eyes. I lifted from the bed and headed into the restroom to brush my teeth and unwrap my hair. Once I was done, we headed out the door, for the doctor. It was only fifteen minutes from the house, so we were there in no time.

We headed inside, and Ru signed my name on the clipboard. I knew we were gonna be here a minute, so he took a seat beside me and let me lean on him to catch some more sleep.

Once again, I was getting into a good sleep, and the nurse called my name. I headed for the back and was instructed to pee in a cup and place it inside an open slot in the wall. Once I was done, I headed back to the front and waited for the results. It only took about twenty minutes, and my name was being called again.

"Ms. Barkley, you're definitely pregnant," the nurse said and slid me the paper with my results.

It described the day I got pregnant and my possible due date. She also gave me a prescription for prenatal vitamins and iron because I was anemic.

Reading over the paper, reality began to set in. I was really having a baby. I turned to look at Ru, and he was happy as hell. After thanking the nurse, we went to the car. Ru couldn't stop smiling, and it made me happy to see his excitement.

I'm really gonna be a mother, I thought, smiling, just as Ru was doing. I looked over at him and wondered if this baby would bring us closer. I mean, we were close, but I still had my doubts about him. I wanted this to be a maturing point of our lives. No more games, no more bitches, and I was gonna do my best to love him.

SEVEN

Amor

"Someone I can spend my life with
Leave the keys to the Benz
Wedding band with the gems
You're someone I feel all right with
Someone to have my kids
The one I can depend on…"
-Next

A few months later

S itting at my desk, I was tearing up a bagel with extra cream cheese. I was now nine months and huge. I still worked at the tax office, but because my boss was cool, she worked with me.

I wasn't ever really sick, but I was always sleepy. Everyone around me made sure to cater to me, which consisted of feeding my fat ass constantly and making sure I didn't have to get up. I had gained so much weight, and other than the constant swelling of my feet, my pregnancy was breezy.

Ru was by my side every step of the way. He was still doing security at the club, so through the night, he was away. I guess the baby helped because we were in a good head space with no discrepancies.

"Amor, you're honey's here."

I looked over at the front desk worker, Erica. Just as I looked out the door, Ru was coming in holding a bouquet of roses. He was smiling from ear to ear as he placed them on the desk. He took a seat with a goofy grin, and we began to make small talk.

"Let me find out you miss me." I took the flowers and began sniffing them.

"Yeah, a nigga miss you. I wanted to holla at you about something."

I looked at him the moment he said it. I frowned. I was unsure about the look he was wearing until he pulled out a small red velvet box. He opened it and looked at me. "So what's up?" he asked, and I guess this was his proposal.

By this time, everyone was surrounding my desk, and even my boss had come out of her office. I began nodding my head *yes,* and he slid the ring onto my finger. I jumped up from my desk and wrapped my arms around him. He kissed me, then rubbed my belly, and the entire office began screaming, "Congratulations!"

After showing my ring off, my boss told me I was excused for the day. I began to pack my things and headed out the door with Ru. We hopped on the highway and headed for the freeway. We pulled up to the beach to a nice restaurant on the water. When we headed in, we were taken to our table, which let me know Ru already had reservations. He pulled my seat out, and this surprised me. I said that because Ru wasn't the affectionate type, and he damn sure wasn't a gentleman. He was a real street nigga, and when it came to him, the streets were his first priority. Maybe the baby was changing him.

"What yo' ass ordering? Lobster, huh?" he asked, chuckling.

He knew me, and I loved some seafood. I nodded *yes* and picked the menu up. I went straight to the seafood section, and, of course, lobster and steak, with a side of king crab, was my choice. Heaven and I couldn't wait to dive in; yes, that was her name. I wished it was a boy, so I could name him after Karter. I missed him so much.

Speaking of, I needed to call my mother because I hadn't talked to her in over three weeks. She was supposed to come down for the baby shower, but she wasn't feeling good. The baby shower was in two weeks, on the beach, and we were having a 'Heaven & Angels' theme.

"Congratulations, Mrs. Simms." A waiter walked over and smiled.

I couldn't help but to smile back because I had to get used to the last name change. I wasn't sure when a wedding would take place, but because he proposed, I was gonna let him handle everything.

"Who's that?" I looked over at Ru because his phone rang three times, and he didn't bother to answer it.

"Oh, that's, Lil' Gee," he replied, referring to his lil' bro.

They weren't really brothers, but because they had grown up together, they were soul bros. Ru's spoiled ass was the only child, and when I say he was spoiled, he was rotten.

"Why you ain't answer?"

"Because this yo' time right now." He slid his phone into his pocket and focused all his attention on me.

I looked at him and fell into a daze. My emotions began running wild, and I couldn't front about my doubts. Things were iffy with Ru. Therefore, I looked at him and...

"You ready for this?"

"For what?"

"For marriage, for this baby?"

"Hell yeah."

"Ru, I mean, this is a big step, and we can move slowly if you want. I'm not rushing you because I want things to be perfect."

"I'm rocking with you, shorty," he replied, and I only looked at him.

I let out a small sigh and prayed I wouldn't be setting myself up for failure. I knew Ru, and to keep shit real, he just didn't seem "into" me. I knew it could've been the cheating because when it came to me, there was no affection. However, I was gonna give it a shot.

"We rocking." He looked at me, and I faintly smiled.

Just as I was about to tell him I loved him, I felt a sharp pain on my side. I grabbed my stomach, and Ru looked at me with concern.

"You good?"

"I don't...ahhhhh!" I started screaming before I could answer. When the pain stopped, I looked at Ru. "I think I'm in labor."

He jumped to his feet in a panic. Another pain hit me so hard it made me fall to the floor, out of my seat. Hell yeah, this was labor. Ru began scrambling around, gathering our things, and when I tried to stand, I felt like I was gonna pass out. I grabbed ahold of the table and tried hard to breathe. I couldn't move, and Ru was forcing me to walk. I shook my head, and all I could do was ask God to make the pain stop.

CHAPTER EIGHT

Chaotic

"I don't know to love
I know I'm down to fuck up
You better put you trust in God
And never put your trust in us..."
-Major Nine

Scrolling through my Facebook page, I stopped at a conversation amongst my sister and a few of her friends. She wasn't my sister by blood, but the hood had us connected. Not only that, her and my lil' bro were now a couple, so we were really tied in. They hooked up while I was locked up, and no lie, the shit blew me back. However, they were a perfect fit for one another because they were tied to each other in so many ways. They both were gangstas, and they both carried my name.

I continued to scroll through her comments, and when I saw the name *Amor Barkley,* I stopped. It was the same little bitch from the video and interest got the best of me. I clicked on her page, and the first thing I spotted was a big ass ring on her finger. Next, I went through the rest of her pictures and read through a few of her statuses. So far, I saw she had a nigga, who I assumed was her husband, because a few of her statuses referred to him as *husband.* Amor and I had over two hundred mutual friends, so I took it upon myself to send her a request.

I wasn't into Facebook, but my little bro set the page up while I was locked up. The first time I logged on, I had thousands of followers and was even tagged in all types of shit. I really wasn't into adding people because I ain't really fuck with people, but being bored with this damn monitor on my leg, I ain't have shit else to do. Last week, I was finally sent home on home confinement, so I couldn't really make any moves. However, everything with my traps were in progress, and one of the houses was already booming.

Amor Barkley Accepted Your Friend Request

I read the message that had popped up on my page, and ol' girl accepted my friend request.

"So you adding bitches now?" I looked up to Ashley, who came out the room.

"Man, what the fuck you talking about?"

"I'm talkin 'bout this Amor bitch. Since when you start adding bitches on social media?"

I couldn't do shit but shake my head because it ain't even been five minutes, and already, I was getting monitored. Over the last two weeks, this had become a regular in this house. It wasn't from adding bitches, but all types of shit had Ash and me beefing. It was like this girl loved to argue, and the more I was here, I was seeing the real her.

"Man, me and that girl grew up together," I lied. Well, I really ain't lie, in a sense, because her and my pops were from the same hood.

"I know where she from, and I know exactly who she is," she shot with a head roll. "Yeah, I had a nigga from over there," she added like I was supposed to get mad.

I ignored her ass and went back to Amor's page, and just that fast, she was deleted. I shook my head and sent her another request. I really ain't give a fuck because wasn't this what social media was for? I mean, I wasn't tryna be social with the bitch. I just added her.

As I continued scrolling, there was a knock at the door. I dropped my phone on the side of me and headed up to see who it was. When I opened it, there was a nigga standing there in a black hoodie.

"Yeah?"

"Ashley here?" he asked, making me chuckle.

I unlocked the door and let the nigga in. Right when I went to call Ashley, she was already coming out of the room. She looked from the nigga to me, then back to him. I headed into the room and slid into my shoes. I wasn't supposed to leave the house, but I ain't give a fuck. I needed to show ol' girl I ain't give a fuck. One thing about me was, I knew how bitches worked, and I didn't give a fuck how much they swore they "didn't do this," or "didn't do that." I ain't trust none.

Once I had my shoes on, I grabbed my strap, then picked up my phone. I walked right past her and ol' boy and ignored her as she began calling my name. I hopped into my rental and headed to my mom's crib. Moms crib was where I was originally home confined to, but I told them people the truth and that I was gonna be at Ashley's.

As I drove for moms, my phone rang nonstop. A few times it was Ashley, but the fifth call was my boy, Remy. I quickly answered because when it came to this nigga, I knew it was money involved.

"Sup, Rem?"

"Sup, nigga? Where you at?"

"Shit, on my way to mom's."

"Oh, you out tonight?"

"Hell nah, I gotta get my ass in."

He laughed, and I knew why. Rem was a young, wild nigga. We did time together in the feds, but the nigga ain't check back in with them people. When he was supposed to go to the halfway house with me, he went on a run and been dodging them people ever since.

"Aye, my homie got this little plug on a gig if you interested. You need that shit, so them people can let you off early," he said, and he was right.

If I followed protocol, I could get off this monitor faster. I really wasn't no nine-to-five type nigga, but to get off this shit, I was with it.

"Hell yeah, I'm down. Just let me know what I gotta do."

"I'mma send you the info in the morning. All you gotta do is go up there."

"A'ight, shoot it to me."

"A'ight. Well, I'll hit you tomorrow. I'm 'bout to go fuck with this little bitch."

"A'ight, stay dangerous." I hung up, and Ashley started calling my phone again. "Man, what's up?"

"I don't know why he came over here. I swear I ain't been fucking with that nigga."

"You good, man."

"Can you come back home?"

"Nah, I'm going to my moms. I got an interview in the morning."

"Wow, so you ain't coming home?"

"Nah," I replied nonchalantly, and when she got quiet, I hung up.

I knew she was in her feelings, but that was her bad. She knew I was on my way home from prison, which gave her time to check her little niggas. Him popping up let me know that was what had been going on, and I be damned if a nigga caught me slipping with my pants down. I had too many enemies in these streets, and it was bad enough niggas knew where I laid my head.

◻

CHAPTER NINE

Amor

"Ooh, I trusted you, I trusted you
So sad, so sad what love will make you do
All the things that we accept
Be the things that we regret..."
-Ashanti

Sitting on the brand new loveseat that I had just purchased, I was holding Heaven in one arm and my cell phone in the other. I was scrolling through my Facebook page tripping off this weird ass nigga who had followed me and deleted me three different times. Keep shit real, I didn't know why he followed me because he was from the other side. I noticed we had tons of mutual friends, so I added him. When I clicked on his page and began scrolling through, it finally dawned on me who he was.

It was Chaotic, who the homies were discussing a few months back in the club. Looking through his pics, I had to admit the nigga was cute as hell with the most beautiful smile. Seeing all the women on his page let me know he was a ladies man, but it ain't mean shit to me because I was a married woman. Well, almost married.

It had now been six months since the day Ru proposed and I went into labor. Not once had Ru mentioned a wedding, and the few times I did mention it, he would brush me off. Things between us were still okay. That was all we were; just okay. I couldn't front. The nigga was a damn good dad, but he lacked in making me happy. He spent so much time at that damn club we barely saw him. When he *was* home, he'd just sleep the days away with Heaven on his chest or spend his free time on his Xbox. I had begun to notice weird shit like him powering his phone off, but I didn't trip. The day I found it in the dirty clothes hamper, on the charger, with laundry on top of it, was the day I started getting suspicious.

The smell of Irish Spring body wash tickled my nose as it came down the hall. This let me know Ru was now up and getting dressed to hit the club. Tonight, I was gonna finally join him and get my first break from my baby. I had already lined up a babysitter because a bitch needed to get out of the house and have a drink. Once I noticed Heaven was asleep, I lifted up from the couch and tiptoed down the hall to lie her in her bedroom. After lying her down, I went into the bedroom, and Ru was lacing his shoes, already prepared to leave.

"I wanna go tonight." I looked at him so he'd know to wait for me.

"Go where, and what you gon' do with Heaven?"

"I got a sitter." I frowned because I didn't like the way he was looking.

"Man, you don't need to go to the club."

"The fuck you mean, 'I don't need to go'?" I replied, getting mad as fuck. This nigga should have been happy I was finally getting up and out.

"Like I said, for what?"

"What the fuck is the problem? I wanna go out, so I'm 'bout to get dressed," I told him, and he walked out the room.

Moments later, he came back inside, and because of his evil facial expression, I stopped and looked at him.

"Damn, you act like it's a problem with me going with you. It ain't never been a problem."

"Mannnn, I ain't even going tonight," he mumbled with an agitated look.

I watched him for a moment, and the nigga looked really mad. I wanted so badly to curse his ass out, but I let it slide. Instead, I just got in my bed, and he sat down at the foot of the bed. He picked up his phone and began texting. He still had an attitude because not once did he look my way. He dropped his phone and stormed out of the room. When I heard his footsteps land in the living room, I quickly jumped up and picked up his phone. There was a fifteen second count down on it, and that confirmed the nigga had a code. However, he left before it locked, so I was able to get in. I went to the first text and the name read *Q*. I began to read the text, and the more I read, I saw red.

Me: *A, shorty, you miss a nigga?*
Q: *What you mean, do I miss you? Nigga, I'm 'bout to see you tonight.*
Me: *Nah, I ain't coming. Some shit came up. I'mma hit you in a min.*
Q: *K.*

There were no other threads after that, which let me know he had deleted them. I quickly went to the number and rehearsed it a few times to remember it. I then jumped up and stormed into the living room and found Ru at the sink washing dishes.

"You bitch ass nigga! You a straight hoe! I swear I'm so tired of yo' shit!" I threw his phone at him and cracked him in the back of his head.

He grabbed his head and looked at me as if I lost my mind. Before I knew it, I started swinging on his ass, and he quickly pinned me down. By this time, I had tears pouring from my eyes, and I was hysterical.

"Man, you need to chill the fuck out." He continued to restrain me.

There was one thing Ru would never do, and that was put his hands on me. I jumped up out of his grip and stormed into the room. I began snatching his clothing out the closet and throwing everything I could into a bag my damn self. Nigga ain't have to pack his shit because I was gonna pack it for him.

As I continued tossing his shit around, he only stood there because he was guilty. I could tell he was trying hard to find the right things to say, but what could the nigga really say? I swear I was more furious because since I had been with him, I really ain't do shit. I was a cold, dog ass bitch, but I was getting older and tired of the games with niggas. Therefore, I gave Ru a chance. On many occasions, I could've dogged him out like I did every nigga before him, but a bitch was living on hope. Hoping one day he'd love me. Hoping one day he'd change. But, hell no. That was all a hopeless lie. Ru was Ru, and even after the proposal, he still wasn't shit. Speaking of, I pulled my ring off and threw it at his ass. I was done.

When I was done packing his shit, I took the bags to my truck, one by one, until I had everything in there. There was nothing left for him to get because everything belonged to me. The house, all three cars, and even the money that was stashed in my bedroom. See that was the part I really never got into about Ru. The nigga did all that working and hustling but left me to carry the weight around the house. He paid a few bills, but everything else I did. I was the one who held us down, and I definitely would be taking full responsibility for my baby.

"Amor, you good?" Tasha walked in and asked.

"No, I'm not. I'm not going out tonight, but I need you to watch Heaven right quick."

She nodded and took a seat. I went outside to the car and waited for Ru to get in. When he came to the car, he had this dumb ass puppy face, but I wasn't buying that shit. I revved the engine and pulled out my driveway doing nearly 100. I was trying to get him there and fast. When I hopped onto the highway, I had a pool of tears running down my face, and he held onto the latch the entire time. I could tell he was contemplating a lie, but he had to think of something good to convince a bitch like me.

The moment we pulled up to his mother's home, he had finally begun to speak his lies. Ignoring him, I jumped out and began sitting the bags on the porch, one by one.

"Man, Amor, that wasn't no bitch. It was the homie." He grabbed my arm, but I snatched away from him.

I stormed back to my truck, and before I climbed in, I turned to look at him. "Nigga, well, I got the number. 583-1212!" He looked at me with a nervous look because I actually remembered the number. "We gon' see if it's the homie. I swear if a bitch answers, it's really over!" I screamed, then pulled off.

The moment I hit the block, he began blowing my phone up. Again, I ignored him because I was already dialing the bitch's number. The phone rang five times, then went to voicemail.

"Hi, you've reached Quincy. Sorry you couldn't reach me, but if you...."

That was all I needed to hear. I hung the phone up just as a message from Ru came through. I pushed my voicemail, and Ru's voice came blaring through my Bluetooth speakers.

"I swear I'm sorry baby girl. I fucked up. Please don't do this to me. To us. Sometimes, a nigga be with the fuckery and not thinking. I love you, and you only. You gotta believe me. I can't let you leave me.

Heaven needs me. Please, Amor. Come back, so we can talk."

I shook my head in disbelief because this nigga had really lost the last part of the mind he had. I swear I was tired of the fake *"I love you,"* and *"I'm sorry,"* and now, he was gonna throw my daughter in it as if I was supposed to feel sorry for him. Nope, not today. I wasn't gonna be this nigga's fool any longer. Or, at least that was what I told myself.

CHAPTER TEN

Chaotic

"Nothin' more, nothin' less but you at my door
Willin' to confess that it's the best you ever tested
Better than all the rest, I'm like, "Aight girlfriend, hold up
I gave you, what you gave me Boo, a nut..."
-DMX

Six months had gone by, and a nigga was working at a trucking company. The pay was good, but not for a nigga like me. I mean, I had to do it to look good for my PO, but I was used to fast money. I could get hundreds of thousands in three minutes, so this shit right here was straight bullshit. Other than that, the job was cool and laid back. It had a gang of ratchet bitches in love wit' a nigga, and I think that was what made it fun.

At this point, Ashley and I were pretty much done, so that gave me the room to mingle a little. A bitch was the last thing on my mind because I was focused on a bag, however, I still needed some pussy. I met this one little chick who was on me heavy. She was slim, but cute. I only fucked with her because I liked her standoff attitude. I was tired of the bitches who always wanted to be seen. When it came to me, I was a lowkey, sneaky ass nigga. I didn't make noise because gangstas moved with silence. The niggas who always made too much noise was the niggas who were straight bitches and them same niggas who always came to get me when shit hit the fan. Therefore, this little bitch was perfect.

"Hey, babe."

I turned around, and Rochell was walking toward me. *Babe?* I thought to myself because baby girl and me weren't even on that type of time. We had been fucking around about four months, but that wasn't enough time to be giving a nigga pet names.

"Sup, Ro?" I wrapped my arm around her for a hug. I let the *babe* shit slide, but if she did it again, I was gon' have to remind her I wasn't the nigga she wanted to take home to moms.

"Hiii, Canyon."

I looked up, and this little bitch, Porsha, was walking by. I hit her with a head nod and smiled flirtatiously ignoring the fact that Rochell was a few feet away from me.

"Damn, you just smiling for girls all in front of me." Rochell watched Porsha walk away.

"Shit, the bitch said hi. You saying something to me about it when you should've checked that bitch."

I frowned because I wasn't the type of nigga to be checked by a bitch. These bitches did this all the time. They ain't respect Rochell, and that shit was a turnoff. I mean, it was okay to be a square, but bitches like her would let a nigga get away with murder. Another thing about me was, I would try my hand, and if you let me get away with it, I would. I ran over bitches like her. I really couldn't do much wit' a chick like Rochell anyway. She lived at home with her pops, so she was just for the moment.

"I'm working the big truck in a couple hours. You gon' slide through?" I smirked as my dick grew in my pants.

"Yeah, if I can. This bitch got me doing a damn oil change."

"What?" I asked, and just that fast, my dick went soft. I knew it was the supervisor, Ms. Jacobs. That was another bitch who was in love with me, and she hated Rochell. Everybody hated Rochell because they were mad I fucked with her heavy. "I'mma holla at that bitch," I assured her. She looked like she was ready to cry and that made me more mad.

"I'll see you later. I gotta go start this bullshit."

"A'ight." I released her and watched her petite frame walk away.

For the next two hours, I ain't do shit. I had to clean the truck, but most of the time I spent in the back asleep. Because they were big rigs, they were equipped with a bed and lots of room to maneuver. No one would ever come looking for me because, like I said, the supervisor was in love wit' a nigga. I waited on Rochell to finish her oil changes, and she had just sent me a text saying she was walking over here. I looked out the window to let her know I was inside. By the time she climbed in, I was already in the back lying on the bed. I pulled my dick from my pants because we ain't have time to waste.

"Take them panties off." I eyed the long dress she was wearing, and clearly, she didn't expect to be doing oil changes.

She walked over to me, lifted her dress, and removed her panties. I slid 'em into my pocket for a keepsake, so her ass was gon' be pantie-less for the day. By the time we finished, it would be time to clock out anyway.

I lifted up from the bed and let Rochell lie down. I lifted her legs in the air and positioned myself between her thighs. Her pussy was nice and shaved, just how I loved it, so my dick went from nine inches to the full eleven. I began using my tip to moisten her up, and before I could get my head in, she was already screaming like I was murdering her.

"Chill. Damn, you gon' get us caught."

"It hurts," she whined, but I ignored her cries.

I slid half of it in and tried hard to find my rhythm. *This bitch gon' get us caught*, I thought, trying hard to focus.

"Ohhhh, shit! Arggggh! Canyon...Canyon! Babe, you hurting me."

Babe? I looked down damn near annoyed. I continued on and started thrusting inside of her. "Damn, this pussy good, ma." I whispered in her ear truthfully.

Because I was the second nigga who'd ever fucked her, her pussy was damn near like a virgin's. The way she always ran from me made me think there was some truth behind it. Lil' mama really couldn't take no dick for real, and her running only made me wanna fuck her harder.

"I think I'm nutting! Ohhhh, shit! Fuckkkkkkk, Canyon!" Again, she began screaming. Now that she got her nut, I was about to focus on mine. However, it was hard with all the screaming she was doing.

After another twenty minutes of killing Rochell, I finally felt the buildup in my nut sack, and I shot every ounce of nut inside her. She was still moaning hard and panting as I continued to release inside her. When I was done, I pulled out and retrieved the towel I already had waiting. Being the fake gentleman I was, I made sure to wipe her off first. Once I was done, I cleaned my dick off and slid back into my clothes. I let her get out of the truck first and waited a few minutes before I climbed out.

When I jumped off, she was standing off to the side waiting on me.

"I'll hit you later," I told her, and she looked at me with a *that's all you wanted* look?

Hell yeah that was all I wanted. I was trying to get the fuck away from her. I fucked with Rochell, but we ain't have shit in common, which left us nothing to talk about. All of our phone conversations were, "I'm on my way," and, "Open the door when I pulled up to fuck."

"Okay..." she replied but didn't move. "Ummm... I was hoping we could maybe go out later or something."

"Go out?" I looked at this girl like she was stupid. "Like on a date?" I asked confused.

"Yes. Movies, dinner, something."

"Nah, ma, I got shit to do. I'll get up with you."

"'K," she replied, and, again, she looked like she was ready to cry.

That shit was aggy as fuck. I didn't know what these bitches wanted from a nigga, but I wasn't the relationship type. I was fresh out and on a come up. I ain't have time for a bitch to be clocking my every move. Shit, I almost slipped up with Ashley, but I dodged that bullet. The only reason I gave Ash a chance was because she held a nigga down in prison. Besides Ashley, I had a fat bitch pulling her weight. That bitch kept my commissary fat, money on the phone, she had great conversation, and she was actually pretty. However, all along, I think I was being catfished by one of the homies' baby mama.

My last ninety days, she sent me a letter saying she did my time, and she wished the best for me. Bitch wrote me a straight *Dear John* letter and left my ass. I ain't gone lie. I was gon' actually pull up on her fat ass, but just like that, she vanished. Deleted her email, changed her number, and went ghost. Shit kinda fucked wit' my ego because a nigga like me ain't never been dumped. I even told the bitch I loved her, but big baby gave me my walking papers.

CHAPTER ELEVEN

Amor

"If you mess with my man
I'mma be the one to bring it to ya
Got my girls, got my man
So find your own and leave mine alone…"
-Nivea

"**A**ye, fuck it up, best friend! Ayyyy!" Misha was yelling on the side of me.

I knew I was good and drunk because no matter where we went, I never danced. Tonight, I was showing out and bringing moves I ain't know I had. I went from twerking to making my ass clap, and my best friend wasn't making shit no better.

Tonight, we decided to hit the club and let our hair down. Knowing we would possibly run into Ru, we decided to go to a club out the way. Since the day I put his ass out, I did my best to avoid him. I didn't go to the hood or nowhere else I knew he'd be. It had been two weeks now, and every day, he text me saying he missed me. A few text I replied to, but for the most part, I left the next on *seen*. I wanted him to know I got his messages and feel stupid.

"Aye, Lady Ru, them Trey Nine niggas up in here," Rawdy leaned over and whispered in my ear.

I began looking around, and it made perfectly good sense why there were blue balloons in the VIP.

"You got yo' pistol?"

"Yeah, but it's in the car."

"Damn," I replied because ain't no telling what these niggas would try and pull.

Although I was now friends with Chaotic on Facebook, and his lady's homegirl and I were cool, them niggas hated my hood and homies.

I continued to scan the VIP, and Lord behold, Chaotic was leaning on the banister looking dead at me. I froze in one place because this was the first time I had seen him in person. We held each other's gaze for a moment until it clicked. He and his homies were deep as fuck, and I didn't trust the nigga. It was definitely time to roll.

Just as I turned around to tell Misha we were leaving, the same bitch from the club Ru worked at, who had been eyeing me, walked by, and she gave me the same look as last time. I didn't know why, but something in my heart told me this was the bitch, Q. I swear it was like a woman's intuition or something because I felt the shit.

"I got a feeling that's the bitch, Quincy." I looked over at my girls.

Misha began staring her down, and before I knew, she walked over to her. I shook my head knowing how things were about to play out, so I followed behind her. Misha's crazy ass was the one who ain't give a fuck. I ain't give a fuck either, but I was a little more level-headed. Rawdy was the same way except she wasn't doing no fighting. She was our shooter and would bust a gun if a muthafucka looked at us wrong.

"You bitches got a problem?" she asked, looking right at me.

"You damn right!" I rushed that bitch so fast she didn't have a chance to defend herself.

I hit her with some powerful blows, and with each one, she stumbled backwards. Suddenly, I felt a hit to the back of my head that made me spin around. Before I could react, Misha had already intervened and was beating her friend's ass. I turned back around, and the bitch and me began fighting again. From that point, I didn't know what happened. It was like I blanked out, and the only thing I remembered next was being lifted off my feet by security and carried outside. Another guard was holding Misha, and Rawdy was on the side of us cursing the security out.

"Either y'all leave, or I'm calling the cops," the security guard said as he put me down on my feet.

The outside was swarming with niggas, and by their appearance, I could tell it was more Trey Nines. I looked at Rawdy, and she was thinking the same thing. There was a large crowd as if some shit was already popping off outside, and before I could figure out what was going on...

"Take yo' ass home, now, Amor!"

"Oh, shit." I turned around to the sound of Ru's voice.

I looked at him and frowned because I wasn't dumb. The nigga was up here to see that bitch. Just as I was about to curse his ass out, all hell broke loose.

Pop! Pop! Pop! Pop! Pop! Pop! Pop! Pop! Pop! Pop! Pop! Pop! Pop! Pop! Pop! Pop! Pop! Pop! Pop! Pop! Pop! Pop! Pop! Pop!

Pop! Pop! Pop! Pop! Pop! Pop! Pop! Pop!

I was quickly snatched to the ground as bullets went flying past my head. While on the ground, I began scanning my surroundings for Misha and Rawdy, and that was when I noticed Ru's little brother on the ground, and he wasn't moving. The crowd had scattered, but I couldn't get to him because bullets were still flying. I saw Ru from the corner of my eyes, and he had his pistol out firing back. Now I wished I had stayed my ass at home.

Chaotic

"**A**in't them the nineteen street bitches?" My lil homie, Gunzo, pulled his strap from his waistband.

I quickly grabbed his arm to let him know to chill because it was Amor. However, that stud bitch with them could catch a few bullets. I hated that bitch because she was too much like a nigga. I swear I was gonna kill her, but in a different time and setting. A nigga had just done all that time fucking with cameras, so this time, I moved different and with sense.

Another reason I didn't jump stupid was because I had found Amor to be pretty cool. After doing a little homework on her, I found out she was a joint in her hood. She had a name over there, but I took it as her past. After skimming through her Facebook page over the last few years, I noticed she was more into her family and her businesses. Despite the face tattoos and the little ghetto that was in her, she didn't strike me as a hood bitch. She cooked daily, spent a lot of time around the house, and seemed like the perfect housewife.

What tripped me out was, where was her nigga? He was never in the background entertaining her, and that was where he was fucking up. A nigga like me would have her ass bent over the stove shoving eleven inches of dick in her. I was never a relationship type, but I always told myself if I did get a girl, she would be the happiest bitch alive. The shit Amor did around her crib was what I always envisioned in a woman. For the most part, she was always just vibing to music and drinking as she moved around her crib.

Believe it or not, I had a romantic side to me. I didn't need it to be a special occasion to drop rose petals. Being raised by my mother and grandmothers, I knew what it was like to be sensual. I knew what a woman craved, and the day I found one, I wanted to attend to her. She was gon' be a happy wife and feeling like that bitch for real.

Bopping my head to Rick Ross' "You The Boss," I walked over to the ledge to take a look at Amor. She was looking bomb as fuck in a little ass hood rat dress, but she possessed class with it, so it didn't look as ratchet. A few times, I watched her body vibrate on the dance floor, and if I didn't know any better, I'd think she was a stripper. Her body in that dress was amazing. Her long legs and plump ass were to die for. She had a pretty bronze complexion with a set of eyes like a Walt Disney princess. They were big and alluring. Her lips fell into a perfect shape, and although she wore weaves, I've seen her real hair out, so I knew she had crop. I ain't gonna lie. She was the baddest thing in my eyes, especially from where we come from, the gutta.

I watched as her mouth moved singing the lyrics to the song. I assumed she felt me watching her because she finally

LOVING A CHAOTIC SAVAGE

looked up, and our eyes met. We held each other's gaze for a moment until a chick walked past that pulled her attention. I continued to watch as things looked pretty heated. They exchanged a few words, and before I knew it, Amor had pieced the bitch. I wanted to run down there and break the shit up, but baby girl wasn't my responsibility. Nine times out of ten, it was prolly over a nigga, so I walked back over to take a seat.

"Mercedes, this my nigga, Chaotic," El introduced.

I looked over at the chick and hit her with a head nod. I assumed he was fucking with her homegirl because he pulled her to the table and bent her ass over. Ol' girl wasn't no amateur either. She tooted her ass in the air and clapped it on him. My nigga, El, was hanging with her, tho', so don't get it fucked up.

Just as I took my seat, the bottle girls walked over with a few more bottles. I took one from one of the chicks and decided to go up straight from the bottle. I sat back on the sofa, and the chick, Mercedes, asked if she could sit down. I nodded for her to go ahead. Shit, this was a free country. I finally got a chance to check her out, and because she wasn't that bad looking, I decided to talk to her.

Fuck it. Wasn't shit else to do. I ain't wanna entertain these hoes who were on me because all of them spent their time shaking ass on the next nigga. To each his own, but I didn't like bitches who spent their days twerking in clubs. And this was another reason I ain't have no bitch.

"Dang, pour me some." Mercedes looked over and smirked as she adjusted her dress.

I watched her thick ass thighs, and my eyes skimmed her entire body. Lil' mama was stacked, with her chocolate ass. She had one dimple and some juicy ass lips that were made for sucking dick.

"There's the cups," I told her because I wasn't her butler.

She grabbed a cup after rolling her eyes.

I poured her some Henn and sat back again to mind my business. *I was gon' keep her company, but this bitch blew it*, I thought, pulling out my phone.

"Damn, you don't talk?"

"What's there to talk about? Talk, I'm listening." I turned in my seat to face her. I wanted to hear this shit.

"You a rude muthafucka." Again, she rolled her eyes.

"I ain't rude. I just don't know you to talk."

"Well, I know you, asshole. I'm Tuck's cousin. I'm always at your park," she said like I was supposed to be happy. Tuck was one of the main niggas hating on a nigga.

"Well, I ain't no park nigga, ma." I took a hit from my bottle. "I run shit, but I do it from afar," I added before hitting the bottle cockily.

"A'ight, cocky ass." She sipped from her cup.

I could tell she liked that cocky shit by the way she smirked. After that, we started chopping it up, and I got more relaxed. We started talking 'bout anything under the sun, and she gave me her number.

"You wanna dance?" she asked, feeling loose from the drank.

"You can come dance on this dick." I sat back.

She stood up and walked over to me. She straddled my lap, and just as she began twerking her ass on me, the sound of gun shots could be heard clearly from outside.

"Watch out." I pushed her off me and jumped to my feet.

CHAPTER TWELVE

Amor

"Wish I knew when the storm came
How many tears did you cry when you lost someone?
We did this shit all for the gutter,
Did this shit for my lil' brother..."
-Meek Mill

Sitting in the hospital with Ru was a sad scene. I never in my life seen a gangsta cry, and the shit was real heart-felt. His little brother wasn't his biological brother, but he had watched him grow up. He started banging at a late age, but he had put in the necessary work to become a name in our hood.

For hours, we thought that it was the Trey Nines who had

killed him, but it ended up being security. I knew after this, the security would definitely end up dead, and the club would be getting shut down.

I looked over at Ru, and he was a wreck. They had just broken the news to us about Akill's passing, and I had to be strong because he was breaking down. The crazier part was, Akill's mother had just passed a couple months ago, so there was no one here but the gang.

Ding!

I looked down at my phone and had an inbox message on Messenger.

Big Chaotic: You straight?
Seen

Amor Barkley: Yeah, I'm straight. Thanks
Seen

I didn't know why, but I smiled.

"They killed my little nigga, man."
I looked up nervously at Ru. I didn't know why I was nervous because I wasn't doing shit. However, I nearly dropped my phone, and he looked at me curiously. Instead of investigating, he had more on his mind to worry about.

"Let's go home." He stood to his feet, then waited for me to stand.

Home? I thought, but I ain't sweat it. Right now, he needed me, so I was gonna be in his corner. I grabbed his hand, and we headed out the door home.

When we got into the car, Ru didn't bother turning on the radio. His phone was blowing up, so it was heard, loudly vibrating. I knew this wasn't the time, but I just had to ask.

"Who's that? Your boo from the club making sure you're alright?"

"That ain't my boo." He kept his head straight as he responded.

"I'm no fool, Ru. I know that's why you were there. I mean, come on. What's the odds of her being at a club across town and you showing up? I'm not stupid, so stop playing me like I am, nigga."

"Look, I know I fucked up, and I'm done with that."

"You fucked her?"

"Nah, wasn't shit like that. I did some frivolous shit by getting her number and damn near lost you in the process."

"Nigga, you always lose me in the process, and that shit never seems to bother you. Ru, one day, you gon' lose me for good, and when I'm gone, ain't no coming back." I turned to look out the window.

I wasn't playing with this nigga. He was gonna lose me, and right when I moved the fuck on was when he was gonna miss me. Just like they said, "You don't miss what you have until it's gone."

❤️🔲🔲

"**T**urn over," Ru told me, so I turned around and tooted my ass in the air. He slid back into me, and only sat there.

I began throwing my ass, and for some odd reason, my pussy wouldn't get wet. This had become a normal, and I couldn't figure it out. I wasn't the type of chick who really got extremely wet for niggas because I never liked a nigga enough to desire them. In all the years of my life, I never had a nigga I craved. It was pretty much a fuck, then I was out. Don't get me wrong, I've been in a couple relationships, but like I said, I didn't desire not one nigga. I tried hard with Ru, but I guess because there was no attraction, there was no satisfaction.

Over the last few months, things had gotten worse. We walked around like strangers, and a part of me felt it was because he was either cheating, or he just wasn't into me anymore. He had begun treating me like I wasn't shit, but no matter what, the nigga stayed in our home and by my side. He played that video game all day and night, while I busied myself in the bedroom. Anytime I'd ask him something, he would snap at me. It was like overnight, he was becoming a damn Grinch, so I kept my distance. The only time he was nice was when he wanted my pussy just like now. I was minding my business on Facebook, and he walked in asking was I hungry. Me agreeing to steak and crab never happened because I ended up bent over our bed throwing my ass back.

"You done?" I asked, wishing he'd hurry up and nut.

"Throw that shit, so I can nut," he replied and began finally fucking me.

I started throwing my ass in a circle, so I could make him quickly nut, and just as I thought, I could feel his leg shake, and his dick began throbbing inside of me.

"Shittt!" I shouted as he released inside of me.

As soon as he stopped, I slid off of him and headed for the shower. Before I hopped in, I went to Facebook and noticed a few comments on my last post. I couldn't help but smile when I saw Chaotic was one of the comments. I ignored everyone's comments and replied to him specifically. We began going back and forth, and before I knew it, I was sitting on the toilet entertained by this nigga for a half-hour. My shower was still running, and I was praying Ru didn't walk in and disturb me. Knowing him, he was prolly asleep.

I set my phone down, and Ru walked right in. I ignored

him and stepped into the shower and let the water run completely over me. Moments later, the door slid open, and in stepped Ru. Again, I ignored him and grabbed my towel, so I could hurry up and soap up. This nigga had just ruined a perfectly good shower. At one point of our life, showers with Ru were exciting. Nowadays, we barely took them, and when we did, it was because we were rushing. I lived for the days he'd bend me over the shower walls and fuck me. Our sex life now had no spark, and there was definitely no chemistry.

"Damn, where you going?" he asked because I was soaped up and ready to step out.

"I'm going to get dressed. You can have the shower, Ru."

"I wanted to—"

"Ain't gon' happen, nigga." I cut him off and rolled my eyes because pussy was the only time the nigga would be fake-nice.

I snatched my towel from the rack and began drying off. Before he could object, I was already out the door. I dried off and slid into my clothes, so he wouldn't get any ideas.

Once I was done, I got into the bed and began watching ESPN to catch the highlights from today's game. The Cowboys played the Steelers, and it was a good game. I didn't bother watching because my team wasn't playing, which was the Raiders. Another thing I enjoyed doing, aside from music, was watching football. I actually liked playing, and before I had Heaven, I'd thought about trying out for the Lingerie League. Of course, Ru was against it, but I still considered it. Now that things were shaky between us, all I had to do was work out a little, and I could join. Since the baby, I was almost back to my normal size, but with the birth control I was taking it kept my weight up.

"You wanna go to a picnic tomorrow?" Ru asked, walking out of the restroom.

"Nah, I'm good."

"A'ight," he quickly replied, and that let me know he ain't

want me to go anyway.

I shook my head and turned to my side, so I could finish watching ESPN. This nigga was a whole joke, and I was so tired of it, so I didn't bother calling him out on it. At this point, Ru had a bitch exhausted with the constant games. I didn't know why, but I felt it in my heart I was gon' leave this nigga for good. I thought that with the tragic death of his brother, and the way I been by his side, he'd be a little more in tune with me, but hell nah. He was right back to that miserable nigga, and, again, the shit was played out.

CHAPTER THIRTEEN

Amor

"Silly of me
Devoted so much time
To find you unfaithful, boy
I nearly lost my mind..."
-Monica

I t was Sunday morning, so I decided to get up and take some oxtails out to cook. On Sundays, I didn't go outside because it was my relax day. I'd cook dinner, watch football, and chill with my baby. Ru had left early to go to the hood, so this was gonna give me a chance to ease my mind.

After taking a quick shower, I slid into my Raiders jersey and some black booty shorts. I then went into Heaven's room, and she was wide awake watching *Mickey Mouse Club House*. I began pulling her clothing from her dresser, so I could bathe her and bring her into the kitchen to eat. Just as I picked her up, my phone began to ring, and it was Misha.

"Hey, hoochie. What you doing?"
"'Bout to bathe the baby, cook, and watch football."
"Who y'all play today?"
"Ugh, Kansas City."
"Aw, they gon' beat y'all ass."
"Fuck you."
We both laughed because KC were some beasts. True, they might beat our ass, but we were the only team in the NFL who could beat 'em.
"So what you cooking?" she asked, and I knew when I said oxtails she was gonna come over.
"Your favorite, so come over, bitch."
"Ohhh, oxtails. I'm on my way. I'll grab a bottle."
"A'ight."
We hung up, and I continued to get Heaven together.

By the time I was done, Misha was at the door holding a bottle of Hennessy in the air. She walked in and went straight to the kitchen to grab the ice and cups. I put Heaven in her highchair and headed into the kitchen to begin cooking. Once I had the meat browned, I began chopping the bell peppers and onions, then dropped everything into the crockpot. I made my way into the living room and took a seat, so I could enjoy my drink.

"Bitch, what got you smiling so hard?"
I looked up from my phone at Misha, who was all in my grill. "Nothing." I smirked and looked back down to my phone.
"Bitch, something got you smiling, so stop playing wit'

me."

I looked up at her again and began giggling. I wanted so badly to tell her, but I was a bit nervous at how she'd react. I bit into my bottom lip contemplating should I just tell her. Misha and I hid no secrets from each other. I mean, anyway, there wasn't shit going on with this boy, so why not tell her?

"I'm laughing at this nigga on my page talking shit about my team."

"What nigga? Spill it."

"Chaotic." I quickly turned my head with a stupid grin.

"Chaotic? What Chaotic?"

"Chaotic from—"

"Trey Nine?" she said before I could finish.

I nodded my head.

"Wait one muthafucking minute. Amor, I know—"

"Noooo, it's nothing like that. We're just Facebook friends."

"And you like the nigga. I could tell by that goofy ass look on yo' face. Ru gon' kill you."

"Fuck Ru, and like I said, we're just friends." I rolled my eyes at the mention of Ru. With all the skeletons in his closet, he was the last person I was worried about.

"That nigga is from our enemy's hood. Do you know how dangerous fucking with him could be? Like, come on, Amor, them niggas have killed our homies, and we've killed theirs. You playing a dangerous ass game." She shook her head and took a sip from her drink.

I understood what she was saying, but she was acting like I was tryna wife the nigga.

"He's cool, Mish, and anyway, we ain't talking 'bout shit but football."

"How did y'all become friends anyway?"

"I been his friend for months."

"Ru gone have a field day with y'all asses."

"Girl, Ru knows what's up with Chaotic. Trust me, he don't want no parts." I curled my lips and rolled my eyes.

It was true. I mean, Ru was a gangsta, but Chaotic was a gangsta who ain't give a fuck. He was one of them niggas who didn't fear shit, and he had proved it in the streets. He had the perfect name because it matched his exact personality.

"Let me see this nigga." Misha snatched my phone and began browsing his photos.

Because he had gone to jail at such a young age, she didn't know what he looked like. Hell, I didn't know what he looked like. I would always hear his name in the streets, and the way they talked about him I thought he was some big black ugly killa. However, that wasn't the case. Chaotic had a copper-colored skin tone that looked like melted caramel. He had dimples to die for and a smile that lit up the sky even when the sun was out.

He stood about five-ten, and to be slender, he looked cut the fuck up under his shirt. His body was covered with tattoos, and the one that got me was the MMG under his eye. He wore his hair in a tapered fade, and the top looked like he brushed it with one of those sponge brushes. When I say this nigga was fine, that was an understatement.

"Damn, bitch, he's fine." Misha looked at me, then continued to scroll through his page. "Who this he tagged in a picture with? His girl?"

"I don't know. Let me see."

I grabbed the phone from her and looked at the picture. It was some thick dark-skinned girl with a long weave. Her Facebook name read Mercedes Allen. I clicked on her page and began looking through her pics. She was a cute chocolate girl but nothing I was worried about. Like I said, I wasn't tryna wife the nigga. We were simply Facebook friends.

I mean, it couldn't go far because not only would Ru lose his mind, but the homies would die. Ru couldn't stand Chaotic, and on several occasions, I've heard Ru mention his name. He was talking to one of our lil' homies, and although the Trey Nines were our worst enemies, I could tell Chaotic had made an enemy of himself.

"So what's been going on with you and Ru anyway?" Misha

asked, bringing my attention from Chaotic's page.

"Girl, he's back on the same shit. I don't know, Mish, it's like the love and affection is gone. He acts like I make him miserable, and I don't understand. If I do, why is he here? I'm so fed up with not being loved. I mean, I could have continued to be the same dog ass bitch I used to be. I gave them streets up to be a damn housewife." I looked at her seriously.

If anybody knew, Misha knew. She knew the dog me, and she saw the new me firsthand. It was like I went from being a carefree girl to a despondent house wife.

"Look what the fuck happened in that club. We fighting and shit over his dirty ass dick."

"We still don't know if that's her."

"True, but I'm sure it's her. If it ain't, it's just some random he's fucking."

"So has he still been fucking with her?"

"He claims he's not, but we both know Ru."

"Well, let's see. Set his ass up."

"How?"

"I don't know. Shit, make a fake text-free number."

I looked off into the air, and Mish was on to something. I knew it sounded foolish, but if you wanted to know what your nigga was up to, you had to investigate.

Taking Misha up on what she said, I created the number and was ready to text.

Text Free: Hey, is this Ruger?
Ruger: Who is this?
Text Free: It's Quincy. I changed my number. What's up with you?
Ruger: Damn, stranger, what's up with you? Wait, how I know it ain't a set up?
Text Free: A set up? Why would I set you up?

Instead of replying, he began calling, and Misha and I tried hard to think of our next plan. We couldn't answer because he knew both our voices.

"We gotta call somebody whose voice he don't know," Misha said, and I began going through my contacts.

When I landed on my old school friend, Tracy, I sent her a text because I knew she'd do it. When she texted back *okay,* that was all I needed to hear. So I called her, then called Ru on three-way. By the time we were done, he had agreed to meet her later, and I was on fire.

"I told you." I looked at Misha sadly, and the nigga proved me right.

He fell right into the trap, and I couldn't do shit but shake my head. I was so out of it I couldn't even focus on my game. Once again, Ru had made a complete fool out of me, and this was routine.

A few hours later, the sun had gone down, and I was good and drunk. It was like I had gotten so obsessed I texted Ru from the fake number the whole day. He called once more, so I had Tracy on the phone again, and I could hear the drunkenness in his voice.

Now, here his drunk ass was, in my house, in my face, like shit was cool. I watched him walk around, and I wanted so bad to crack him upside his head, but I kept my cool. When he walked to the back of the house, toward our bedroom, I quickly sent him a text.

Text Free: *Hey, I'm ready. Wya?*
Ruger: *I came to the house real quick. Meet me at the gas station on Main & Central.*
Text Free: *Okay. I'll be there in about thirty minutes. We can go to*

my house from there.
Ruger: *Fasho.*

I quickly dropped the phone when I heard his footsteps approaching.

"Where you going?"

"Why? I got shit to do." He frowned like I was irritating him.

"You been gone all day. I thought you were staying with us?" I asked with tears threatening to fall. I couldn't believe this nigga.

"I gotta go drop off some weed, then slide to the hood," he lied, looking me dead in the eyes.

"Okay," I replied, and just like that, he was gone.

I wanted so badly to follow him to see if he was really going, but I decided against it. I would definitely catch a case tonight, and at this point, Ru wasn't worth it.

CHAPTER FOURTEEN

Chaotic

*"Northern Cal on my shoulders, this shit a lot of weight
The blemishes in my eyes show a lot of pain
One up top, catch a body gang
How could you fault me for my wrongs? This was how I was raised..."*
-Mozzy

Lying back on my bed, I skimmed through Facebook look-ing for one person and one person only; Amor. As much as I wanted to hate baby girl, I couldn't because some-thing about her personality had a nigga intrigued. Like always, she was in the kitchen, and her nigga was nowhere around.

These last couple months, we had been flirting, and I used football as an excuse to make her talk to a nigga. When I found out she was a Raiders fan, that was all I needed. I was a diehard Dallas fan, and our teams hated each other, so this was perfect. I ended up making an Instagram page, and I followed her. Not even ten minutes later, she followed back, and that told me she was crushing on a nigga.

All this social media shit was bullshit to me, but fraternizing with Amor kept me on here. I'd find myself throughout the day checking my pages to see if she either hit me or replied to some slick shit I'd say in her comments. On a few of her posts, her nigga was in the comments, but I didn't give a fuck. I mean, we wasn't doing shit but talking football, right? However, I knew Amor prolly was going through it because the nigga, Ruger, hated me. We've had several shootouts on many occasions, but that was before I got locked up. I didn't know where the nigga head was now, and for Amor's sake, I was gonna chill.

"Sup?" I answered my phone for Mercedes.

"I'm on my way."

"A'ight, I'm waiting on you."

I hung up the phone and lifted from the bed to slide my shirt on. Tonight, we were going to a bar to catch Monday Night Football, and, of course, my team was playing. We were playing the Eagles, and I had a couple hundred-dollar bets. I couldn't believe it, but Mercedes was tagging along, so I guess you could call it a date. Since the night of the club, I decided to give her a call, and to my surprise, she was cool.

A week later, I had her bent over in my crib, and her little pussy was decent. I couldn't front, though. The bitch was a cold freak, and this was another bonus. We had been kicking it tough lately, and she was actually somebody I could fall back on. The only thing was, she was starting to act like my girl, which had me wondering if I was ready for a relationship.

When it came to relationships, I wasn't a cheating ass nigga. Therefore, I wasn't sure if I was ready. Mercedes did everything I needed her to do without asking, and she was beginning to grow on me, but I was still unsure. I was still fucking Rochell from time to time, but I couldn't get past the fact that she couldn't take no dick. I mean, her pussy was good, but I was a nasty nigga, so I needed a nasty bitch to match my energy.

After twisting my cap to the back, I threw my shirt over my shoulder and headed for the front. Mercedes was already on the porch about to knock on the door.

"I gotta pee." She was bouncing around, so I let her in to use it. "I need to change my shoes too!" she shouted over her shoulder as she ran for the bathroom in my bedroom.

I headed into the room and waited for her to come out. She opened the closet door and put on a pair Tory Burch sandals she had left in the closet. I noticed she had been leaving all types of shit around my crib. I ain't sweat it because I didn't have bitches over here anyway. I ain't trust these hoes, and she was lucky I made an exception with her.

"You ready?"

"Yeah, let's go."

We headed for the car and climbed in. I entered the location of the bar into my GPS, and we headed for the highway.

When we pulled up, I noticed all the exotic cars, and the place was packed. One of my homies was inside watching the previous game, so we had seats already waiting for us. After bypassing security, we went and found Mayor, who was at the bar with a plate of wings in front of him, along with an oversized glass of beer.

"Chaotic, what up, my nigga?"

We slapped hands as Mercedes took a seat. I noticed she didn't speak, and I assumed Mayor caught wind of it because he zoomed in on her.

"What's yo name?"

"Mercedes."

"Well, I'm Mayor, Mercedes. I'm his muthafucking dawg, and I could be your worst nightmare."

Mercedes frowned, not knowing what he was talking about.

"You take care of my boy, or I'll haunt you in your dreams," he added, and she giggled.

Little did she know, this nigga wasn't playing. Mayor was my older homie, and he had watched me grow up from a pup. I've always heard stories of his gangsta growing up, but now that I had gotten older, I saw the shit firsthand. The nigga was a stone cold killa, and people around him who ain't no him would never believe it. He was like an angel in disguise type of a nigga because his persona was sort of a businessman but laid back. That shit had cap. This nigga would lay the whole place down and execute the entire room if they dared to object to his command.

"Nah, I got him." She slightly rolled her eyes and threw her hair behind her head on some cocky shit.

That little cocky shit turned me on, but it wasn't called for all the time. This nigga was serious as a heart attack, but she thought he was bullshitting.

I took my seat, and Mayor and I began chopping it up until the game came on. The entire time, I was watching my surroundings and sizing shit up. It was so much money in this bar the shit would be an easy lick. They had one guard by the door and one inside the establishment who didn't pose as a threat.

"Don't even think about it, nigga." Mayor looked at me and took a gulp of his beer.

"Man, stall me out." I chuckled because this nigga knew me like a fucking book. "I ain't gon' lie. Shit easy too, big homie."

"Hell yeah, it's some bread in here. This my homie's spot. Nigga racked up."

"That's yo homie, not mine," I replied seriously.

Mayor ain't say shit because he knew what type nigga I was. I didn't follow rules. I was my own man, and just because I soaked up game from my older homies, I still ran my own shit. □

"You see that one over there at that table?" Mayor said and pointed with a head nod.

"Yep," I responded in a low tone as I glanced ol' boys way.

"That's his brother, Raphael. He the nigga holding. Keep bands in his crib because the nigga ain't got a green card, so he can't get bank accounts."

I didn't reply, but I took in everything he was saying.

"Can I get you two any drinks?" the bartender walked over and asked.

"Yeah, let me get a double shot of Remy. What you want?" I asked Mercedes, who sat on the other side of me quietly.

"I'll take an Adios."

"Coming right up." The bartender scurried off to begin making our drinks.

I looked up at the screen, and it was flashing the previous scores. When I saw that the Raiders had lost, it made me think of Amor. I pulled out my phone and went to her Facebook.

I looked up just in time to catch Cooper scoring a touchdown. Everyone who was a Dallas fan in the building began screaming.

"Aww, nigga, y'all still ain't gon' win." Mayor was on some hater shit. His team was the Seahawks, and they had already lost.

"Nigga, just have my money ready."

I hit my cup as soon as she set it down. I then picked up the menu and began browsing it for food. From time to time, Amor and I went back and forth on social media, and the entire time, Mercedes was watching. I could sense the slight attitude when she noticed I was talking to a female. I didn't pay her ass no mind because she wasn't my bitch, and this was something that was going on before her.

J umping to my feet, because we had just scored the last touchdown of the game, a nigga was hyped. There was only two minutes left in the game, and they were down two touchdowns and a field goal. It wasn't no coming back for them. I collected my bread from Mayor, and we all got up to head out.

When we got outside, I noticed a Lamborghini parked out front, so I looked at Mayor. When he nodded his head, I knew then the car belonged to Raphael. I slid into my pocket as if I was looking for the keys and pulled out the device I kept on me.

"Dang, you drunk." Mercedes laughed when I bumped into her and knocked her purse off her shoulder.

"My bad, ma," I apologized and bent down to grab her purse.

While I was on the ground, I quickly stuck the device under Raphael's whip and lifted up like nothing. I knew I said I was done with the life of crime, but a lick this easy was too hard to resist. Shit was easy, especially compared to trapping. Although my traps were booming, that trap boy shit was too slow compared to the fast money I was used to.

"We going to your house?" Mercedes asked as we got into the car.

"Yeah," I replied and adjusted my music.

"Okay, I just wanted to let Darlene know," she replied, speaking of her babysitter.

"Let's just go get her."

I made a U-turn and headed for the sitter's crib. I had only met Mercedes' daughter twice, and already, I fell in love with her. She was six with a crazy ass personality. The first day I met her, she jumped straight into my arms and began asking me a million questions. When she asked was I her mother's boyfriend, I didn't even know what to say, so I replied *yes*.

We pulled up to the sitter's house, and Mercedes headed in to get Mecole. I used this as time to call my lil' brother. On the second ring, he answered, and his background sounded lit.

"Bro, where you at? Its lit over here."

"Just left the bar. Where y'all at?"

"We at Mama Trey house. It's her granddaughter's birthday."

"A'ight, I got Mercedes and her daughter with me. I'mma pull up."

"A'ight, I'm right here."

I hung up and waited for Mercedes to come out of the crib.

"Chaotic!" Mecole ran full speed toward the car screaming my name.

I couldn't help but laugh because no matter how many times I told her to call me by my name, she would call me my street name. "Hey, baby girl. You had fun?"

"Yes! We went to the movies and look at what I got." She held up a stuffed unicorn.

"Aw, that's dope. You wanna go to a birthday party?"

"Ohhh, yeah," she said and buckled her seatbelt.

Mercedes walked out and got back into the car, so we headed for the party.

CHAPTER FIFTEEN

Amor

*"I am finished cryin' over your lyin', over
denyin', I am so over you, so over you
Said I'm finished with it, ain't no more hurtin' over here..."*
-Ashanti

Since the day I fake-texted Ru acting like I was Quincy, everything in our relationship was bad. I was side-eyeing the nigga every time he walked out the house, which was all the time. Two could play that game because I started leaving all the time too. Whenever Ru decided to leave, I would make him take my daughter. I spent a lot of my days with Misha and in the hood. I would hang on blocks I knew Ru wouldn't come to, but really, I wasn't worried because he was spending his time on the Westside.

Things with Chaotic and I had begun heating up because we had started flirting more. We still hadn't talked on the phone or anything, but we did move from commenting on post to inbox-messaging. I was in my feelings a little bit because he had started posting his girlfriend, Mercedes, more. They were always out on cute little dates, and he even posted who I assumed was her daughter. If you asked me, his girlfriend was better than me because it had gotten so bad with us the nigga started tagging me in post. Therefore, I started tagging his ass too, but we kept it strictly about football.

"What's up, bitch! We out tonight?" Misha yelled into the phone the moment I answered.

"Yeah. I gotta go to work for a few hours. Soon as I clock out, I'll hit you."

"Okay. I get off at three today, so hit me."

Beep! Beep! Beep!

"Okay." I rushed her off the phone because Ru was calling. "Yeah?" I asked, unbothered by his call.

"What's up with you and this nigga on Facebook?"

"What the fuck you talking about?" I played dumb. I had deleted Ru on all my social media, so he wouldn't be in my business, however, someone told the nigga anyway.

"You and this Trey Nine nigga."

"We're just Facebook friends. That's it that's all, and, nigga, you got your nerves questioning me."

"Delete him."

"No, I'm not deleting him. Delete all yo' bitches." I fumed because this nigga had tons of his exes on his page.

"I don't need muthafuckas calling me, telling me my bitch flirting on Facebook with one of my enemies."

"And I don't need people telling me my nigga liking his ex

bitches' pictures on Facebook either." I rolled my eyes, and he got quiet. "Exactly. Bye, Ru."

I hung up on him and went to his Facebook page. I began skimming through his page and laughed when I saw he added Chaotic's girlfriend, Mercedes, as a friend. *This nigga so childish, I swear*, I thought as I slid into my shoes.

I headed out the house and climbed into my car to head to work. Lord knows I didn't feel like being there, but I didn't have a choice. I had to audit a few files to get them ready for an IRS audit. I turned on my music and went to my YouTube app. I didn't know why, but today, I wasn't in the mood for my normal morning oldies.

"Time and time, I try to leave
But I just can't seem to leave yo' ass alone
Don't know why I can't let you go
And why I keep comin' back for mo'..."

I began singing the lyrics of Young Buck's "U Ain't Going Nowhere." I had an entire concert to myself as I vibed on my way to the office. One thing I enjoyed was music, and it always put me in a good mood. I wasn't really into rap, so I always listened to oldies. Anita Baker was my favorite, and I loved me some Teena Marie. I had their whole catalog, and I never got tired of either of their music.

I swerved into my job's parking lot and hopped out to head inside. I was already ready to get this day over with, so I could go hang out and get fucked up. I only had to work until two today, so I was grateful. When I made it through the doors, I was greeted by the front desk worker, Erica. I spoke back and grabbed the clipboard from her hand. I began looking through the names to see if any of my clients had come, and there were three. I began looking around the busy lobby and motioned for them to give me a moment.

When I heard someone smack their lips, it made me look over, and Lord behold; it was Quincy. Well, I still wasn't sure if that was her, but I was certain. However, today would be the day to find out. I continued to browse the sign-in, and there it was there: *Quincy Clark*. I nodded my head once and dropped the clipboard. I mugged the bitch one last time and went to my desk.

"Erica!" I called her name, and she came over. "Who that bitch here for?" I pointed to Quincy, who was now looking agitated.

"She's here for the boss. She filed at another one of our locations and was having issues with a loan."

"A'ight," I replied and dismissed her.

I powered on my computer and began logging into our system. The entire time, I couldn't get the shit off my mind. Ru had never admitted it was her, but because he didn't deny it, I still had the feeling. I swear I was so done with that nigga. It was the disrespect for me. Like, damn, you take me to a club with you and have the nerve to meet a bitch; while I was there. Ugh, I knew I wasn't gonna be able to get through this day with a clear mind, but I was gonna try. As long as this bitch was in my presence, it would be worse, so I prayed like hell they would hurry and get her the fuck out my face.

J ust like I said, the day went by slow, and a bitch was in her feelings. Ru called me several times, but I didn't bother to answer. It was now 1:50 p.m., so I clocked out and began packing up early. This shit really made me wanna get out tonight, and who knows. I might find some dick to lay up with because Ru wasn't it no more.

For so many years, I had enough respect for the nigga not to sleep around, although he had cheated numerous of times. That shit was over with. It was on, and I swear I was gonna cause him so much grief he was gon' need a Perc to stop the pain.

With all the traffic in the streets, I made it to Misha's twenty after three. Because she only lived about a mile away, she was already home, so I grabbed my slut bag and headed in to re-shower. I wanted to slide into something a little more ratchet because I was wearing jeans and a blazer.

"You ready, bitch? Because we going up tonight!" Misha squealed, holding up two fifths of Henn.

"I'm ready." I smirked and dropped my bag.

I wanted to tell her about the bitch, Quincy, coming to my job, but I was gonna save that for the car ride to the hood.

❤️□□□

"Ayyyyyye! Get it!" Like always, Misha was on the side of me pumping me up. She got a kick of me twerking because I never danced.

I was good and drunk, and we had the block lit.

"Yo' thick ass gon' pay for the hood of my car if you dent my shit!" the homie, Bo, yelled toward me.

I was on top of his car, shaking my ass, so when I say I was lit, I was lit. I laughed at him and jumped down, then continued on with my entertainment. There were so many people out tonight from bitches across the tracks to niggas all the way out the 80s. There was a huge dice game going on, and we had so many bottles. One thing about my bitches and I, we didn't wait for niggas to come around and buy us liquor. We bought bottles after bottles and didn't stop until our bodies couldn't consume any more.

When we first got here, I was a little saddened because this was my old street up until my mother moved away. About fifteen feet away from me was where my little brother was murdered, and this was another reason I had gotten so damn drunk. I hated coming on this block, but because this was where everyone was, I didn't wanna ruin the fun for my girls.

"Aye, y'all be safe. I'm 'bout to go fuck with Resina." Rawdy looked down at her watch.

"What time is it?" Misha asked because she had to be at work at eight.

"It's 3:19," Rawdy replied, followed by a yawn.

It was three in the morning, and we were lit like it was two p.m.

"We 'bout to go too." I looked at my girls.

"Y'all go crash in my room until the morning," Rawdy said and pulled out her house keys.

It was actually perfect because Misha was yawning too, which told me she didn't feel like driving. I took Rawdy's keys, and we told everyone we'd see them later. We climbed into Misha's BMW and headed one block over to Rawdy's crib.

When we walked in, we headed straight for Rawdy's room trying hard not to wake her grandmother. Ms. Sinclair was cool, however, she was the type who would start cooking and offering us food at this time of the morning. That lady ain't care what time of the night it was; her generosity ran deep.

"Yo ass sleeping by the wall." I slid out my shoes and let Misha climb in bed first.

Her tired ass ain't reply. She just lay down and turned towards the wall. I lay down and pulled out my phone. For the first time in a long time, I checked my Snap, and my heart dropped when I saw a request from Chaotic. I accepted the request and instantly began watching his stories. The last one was posted about ten minutes ago of him dressed in an orange work vest. His caption read *Workflow. Good morning, Snap.* I didn't know why, so I'mma blame it on the liquor, but I sent him a message.

Snapchat
Me: *Is you working hard or hardly working?*
Chaoticthegreat: *I'm on my way now. What's up with you?*
Me: *You.*

Ten minutes passed...

I started to bite my bottom lip praying I didn't run him off. He didn't reply, and now I regretted saying the shit. Suddenly, his emoji man popped up, and I could see he was writing.

Chaoticthegreat: *Damn, is that right?*
Me: *Yes.*
Me: *Can I tell you something?*
Chaoticthegreat: *Go ahead, ma.*
Me: *I think you're really cute, and I like you. I've been liking you for a while.*
Me: *I just didn't know how to tell you.*

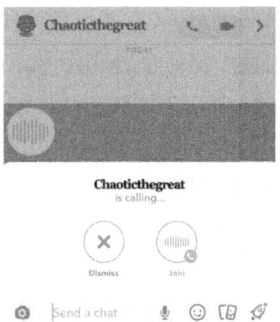

Instead of replying, Chaotic began calling me on video chat. I was so damn nervous I let the call end, and he began calling again. *Oh, lord.*

"Hey," I answered without my face in the camera.

"Bring yo' face to the camera," he demanded rudely, and I did as told. "What's up with you?"

"Nothing, just got in."

"Oh, okay." He paused for a brief moment. "So you like me and think I'm cute, huh?"

"Yes." I nodded my head shyly. I swear to all the Gods, I had butterflies, somersaults, and the bubble guts happening in my stomach all at once.

"So why you ain't never said shit?"

"I don't know. I guess...I guess because..."

"I'm from the other side?" He smirked into the camera, and, boy, was this man fine. Even with his serious face, I could still see the huge dimples that complemented his cheeks.

"Well, that too. And because you got a girl. I don't like stepping on people's toes."

"Shit, you got a nigga," he replied, and I left it at that.

I wanted to say fuck Ru, and he could eat my ass, but I left it alone. "True, but you look happy."

"Well, looks can be deceiving. What's up with you, tho'?" he asked, and from there, the conversation just flowed.

Thirty minutes later, he pulled up to work and told me give him ten minutes because he was going to clock in. Exactly ten minutes later, he called me back, and we spent the entire morning on the phone.

During one period of the call, I heard a female voice in the background asking if they were going to lunch. I then heard Chaotic tell her, *nah, not tonight,* and he returned to the phone as if it was nothing. A part of me got jealous, but I let it go, not wanting him to know. We began talking about all kinds of things, and before I knew it, the sun was peeking through the blinds, and I had learned so much about him. I swear this nigga's conversation was even better than I thought. I found myself crushing on him, and hard. Ru hadn't crossed my mind once, but I wasn't gonna get my hopes up. He had a girl, and like I said, I wasn't into stepping on bitches' toes. *Sigh.*

❤️□□□

By the time I walked into my home, it was 7:26 a.m., and I hadn't gotten any sleep. Ru was in the living room playing his game, but we didn't say a thing to one another. I headed down the hall for my bedroom and lay right down.

After that conversation I had with Chaotic, the nigga was heavy on my mind. I couldn't shake the thoughts of him to save my life, and he wasn't making shit any better. The attention he was giving me was making me crave his ass more, and already I couldn't wait until he called me back. I knew in my heart I was playing a dangerous game, but the lust demon was eating away at me. He didn't seem like the monstrous man the streets painted him out to be. He was actually sweet and definitely a gentleman. I didn't know where we were going with this, but what I did know was, I would have to end it because of the circumstances. He was an enemy, and the whole hood would die, and that was just how it was.

I lived in the shadow of my homies, and when I say they treated me like a Princess, that was what it was. Everyone was able to do as they pleased, but when it came to me, them niggas acted like they were the ones I was fucking. No scratch that; they acted like my daddy, and I didn't even have one of those.

My father split when my mom was pregnant with me. He tried to reach out when I was about seven years old by calling three-way with his new bitch. Nigga had gotten locked up and thought my mom would give a fuck. He was wrong. My mom hung up on his ass, and after three more attempts, he never tried again. The closest thing I ever had to a father was Karter's dad, but he died in a fire six months after Karter was killed.

I knew that was another reason why my mother moved away, and I could say I didn't blame her. The way Ru had me feeling, I wanted to pack my daughter and me up and move out there with her. Wasn't shit out here for me but Rawdy and Misha, and they would be the only thing I'd miss.

CHAPTER SIXTEEN

Chaotic

"I'm just saying you could do better
Tell me have you heard that lately?
I'm just saying you could do better
And I'll start hatin' only if you make me..."
-Drake

"So what you gonna do because I lost my job?" Mercedes looked at me sadly.

It was my fault because I had her late numerous times, and she had started taking days off. Keep shit real, I didn't want her working anyway. My bitch didn't need to work, and since she had stepped up to become my bitch, it applied to her too.

"Shit, rob." I looked at her seriously knowing she would start tripping.

She tilted her head, then looked at me to see if I was serious. "Robbing? Is that what you do?"

I nodded my head *yes* because I didn't really know how to answer that. She knew about me going to jail for robbing the casino, but I never admitted that was a nigga's hustle.

"I have a few trap houses in the hood, but that's slow money. The shit I do brings in about fifty-k or more, depending."

Her eyes buckled when I said fifty-k, and I made sure to make a mental note of that. When it came to women, I paid attention to signs.. Even if I didn't call you out on it, I'd let the shit build up.

"But what if something happens to you?"

"It won't. Trust me."

"Well, if that's what you do." She shrugged.

That was another thing to add to the list. A bitch who loved you wouldn't want you in harm's way, and this bitch had just agreed to let me put my life on the line. I mean, I was gon' do it anyway, but, damn.

"So when are you going out?" she asked, and I looked at her steadily.

I was trying hard to read her, and just that fast, I knew what type of bitch she was.

"Tonight."

I lifted from the sofa and headed into my room. I really ain't have anything left to say. I needed to clear my head about this lick, and Amor was the person to do it.

Snapchat

Me: *What's up, Cute Face? Wyd?*

Fifteen minutes later.

BrothatsAmor: *Hey ☺ At work.*
Me: *Is that right? So where you work at?*
BrothatsAmor: *At a tax office on Broadway and 1ˢᵗStreet.*
Me: *Damn, I pass by there almost every day.*
BrothatsAmor: *Why? One of yo boo's live over here?*
Me: *Nah lol. My moms stay that way.*
BrothatsAmor: *Oh, okay.*

She replied back, and I was already putting my hat on. I walked out my bedroom and told Mercedes I'd be back. She looked at me already knowing what I was on. No, "Be safe." No, "I love you." Nothing. I mean, I knew we weren't together long, and even if I didn't love the bitch, she could have said something. Shit, I was doing this for her too. She lost her job, bills had to get paid, and her daughter liked new iPhones at only six.

I jumped into my whip and headed for Broadway. I had so much on my mind I needed to see ol' girl. I knew there were chances I could possibly run into her nigga or something, but I didn't give a fuck. Amor was mine already; she just ain't know yet. This lil' bitch had me thinking 'bout her when I knew I wasn't supposed to. I had just started a relationship with Cedes, so I wasn't supposed to crave another woman. However, Amor was the perfect fit in what I saw as a wife. Right now, I was a man on a mission, so I couldn't give her all of me. Therefore, I wasn't gon' play games with her until I was ready.

"I know you really, really want it
But you belong to somebody else
Both, wanna be together
But we can't act on it…"

The entire way to Amor's job, I listened to Dej Loaf & Jacquees' "You Belong To Somebody Else." I pulled out my phone and began recording a snap. I sent it to Amor, and she replied within seconds with her usual blush face. She began typing, but

I dropped my phone into the cupholder because I was out in front of her job. I climbed out the car eager as fuck to see her.

When I walked in, there was a girl at the receptionist desk, who tried to stop me from walking to her desk, but I bypassed her. Amor had her head down looking through a bunch of papers, and when she heard the front desk bitch's voice, she looked up. At first, she looked shocked to see me, then she smiled wide. I invited myself to have a seat and waited for her shy ass to speak. She was blushing hard as hell, damn near hiding her face.

"'Sup, Cute Face?" I smirked, knowing she was nervous.

"What you doing here?" she asked, still smiling.

"Came to see yo' sexy ass," I replied, and she got up from the desk and went to the front desk. She came right back holding a clipboard and slid it in front of me.

"Fill this out, so it will look like I'm working."

"Don't be using me, ma."

We both laughed.

I grabbed an ink pen from her cupholder and began filling out the form. We chatted briefly, but not too much because her ass was too damn nervous.

"Canyon Betterman. Nigga, you put yo real name on here?" She giggled.

"Yeah, shit." I stood to my feet.

She looked up at me, and I could tell she was wondering why I stood.

"Where you going?"

"Damn, you don't want me to leave?" I chuckled.

"Nooo...yeah...shit, yes. I don't know why yo' ass came anyway."

"Yeah, a'ight." Again, I chuckled and didn't even reply to her bullshit. "I'mma get up with you."

I headed out the door. Little did she know, I ain't wanna leave her either, but I had shit to do. Like I said, I was a man on a mission with my hand on my gun.

❤️□□□

The moment I got into my whip, my phone began ringing. I knew it wasn't Amor because she ain't have my number. We only communicated on social media, and that was out of respect for Mercedes. Speaking of, it was her calling, and a part of me ain't wanna answer.

"'Sup?"

"Who belongs to somebody else?"

"Huh?"

"Yo' video. Who that's for?" she asked again, and I finally caught on.

"It ain't for nobody," I replied agitated. *Here we go with this bullshit,* I thought and pulled off from Amor's job.

"Yeah, a'ight. I'll see you later."

She hung up, and I couldn't do shit but chuckle. No, "Be safe," or "Good luck." Nothing, once again. Not that I needed it, but, damn. If she was tryna gain that position and secure it, she needed to show concern.

I pulled right up to my nigga Remy, and like always, he was arguing with his little chick, Jewels. Jewels was from Amor's neighborhood, and to my surprise, she fucked with Remy. He wasn't from my hood, but he was affiliated with the Crips, and where I came from, that shit was a no-no.

"Man, hurry up and get me from around this bitch." He climbed in breathing hard.

I pulled off, and she was still cursing his ass out. He had a few scratches on his neck, and his shirt was ripped at the collar.

"Nigga, you in the middle of the enemy's hood fighting

this bitch. Fuck wrong with you?"

"Man, that bitch crazy."

"You in love with her little ass."

"That's my bitch." He didn't deny it, so I laughed.

Remy liked that wild shit. Me? I was a laid back nigga, so fighting and shit was out. Especially when it came to yo' chick. ꘎ I dealt with too much in the streets, so if I had to come home and deal with that crazy shit too, I would leave.

"Where you coming from?"

"Amor's job."

"You talking 'bout me, nigga. You the one in love with that bitch."

"Watch yo' mouth." I looked at him seriously.

"See." He shook his head. Because if anybody knew I ain't love these hoes, it was him. However, Amor was different. Don't ask me why because I didn't know. "So what we on?"

"We 'bout to hit this nigga." I slid him my other phone that was following the tracker.

He watched it briefly, then nodded in agreeance. We had about another two hours before the sun went completely down, and it was time. I looked at him, lost in my thoughts, and I didn't know what made me say it, but I confessed.

"When we hit for a bag, I'm going to get Amor."

"Come on," he replied.

He knew the situation with Cedes, but he knew how I felt about Amor. This was the only nigga I really had to talk to, so he knew it all. I meant exactly what I said too; I was going to get my bitch. I just needed to pass on some major money, so I could sit my ass down. Amor didn't strike me as the type to let a nigga live wild in these streets. The shit I was doing was different from her nigga. After doing my homework on her, I knew she was into hustling and had now settled down. She had a gun case and was on a joint suspension. My lil' baby was a criminal. I smiled thinking about her.

"What you gon' do about ol' girl?" he asked, referring to Cedes.

I thought long and hard before I answered. I looked at him and began to tell him how I felt. I told him about today, and it tripped my young nigga out.

He shook his head and looked at me. "Well, my nigga, it's time you go get yo' bitch."

CHAPTER SEVENTEEN

Amor

"Now what am I supposed to do
When I want you in my world
But how can I want you for myself
When I'm already someone's girl..."
-Erykah Badu

O ver the course of two months, Chaotic and I talked every day, all day on Snap. If we weren't on Snap, then he would pop up to my job unannounced. I swear this nigga would come into the place like he owned the world. He was cocky as hell, and a complete asshole to everyone around us.

Not only around us, but I noticed how he talked to people

on Facebook, and I could only imagine how he acted in public. This nigga was as chaotic as his name, and it fit him perfectly. However, when it came to me, he was pleasant.

I didn't know why, but when I looked in his eyes, I saw the ton of bricks the world caused on his shoulders. Yet, there was something tranquil about the peace in his eyes when he sat at my desk. The shit was a trip because he reminded me of the Joker. He would terrorize the entire world, and the only thing in the world he loved was Harley Quinn. Not saying he loved me, but our eyes spoke to each other. I really never understood why he looked so broken because his love-life looked perfect, and the way his girl-friend shopped, I knew their finances were straight.

It had come to a point where I stopped watching his Snap story because I was jealous of the constant rose petals he dropped to her feet. The many trips to Atlantic City, and especially when they lay in bed making out. That was why I didn't understand why he seemed so into me. He looked happy with her, and that was where he needed to stay and leave me the fuck alone. I was finding myself falling for this nigga, and the shit was playing with my mental and emotions. The more he came around, I found myself intrigued. I spent too many days and nights day dreaming about a nigga I wasn't supposed to.

Meanwhile, I had begun running from my problems at home. I left daily to escape Ru. For some odd reason, the nigga had been spending so much time around the house. We barely talked, and it was like our sex life had completely stopped. Like I said, I was always in the streets with a bottle of Hennessy nestled in my hands and a blunt between my lips. If I were home, I'd stay cooped up in my room with my baby. The energy in our house was so bad the shit was taking a toll on me. It was like Ru was trying to prove a point to me but stressing himself out in the process. That nigga loved them streets, and it was killing him not going out.

"Hey, booooooo!"

I looked up, and my co-worker, Jami, did a little dance as she walked into the office.

"Jamiiii!" I jumped from behind my desk and ran over to hug her. "What you doing here?"

"Girl, I'm back. They sold our building, so I'm gonna be working here with you again."

"Good, because it's gonna start getting busy again soon."

"Is Rosie here?"

"No, she really hasn't been here much."

"Okay. Well, I guess I'll take my old desk." Jami began putting all her belongings on the desk next to me. "What you doing tonight?" she asked, looking over at me as she loaded her stapler with staples.

"Nothing, turning the fuck up."

"Oh, okay. I'm going to my homebody's studio. You should come. It be lit in that bitch."

"I'm down. I just gotta go home and check on the baby. I'mma get dressed and call you."

"Okay, cool."

My phone began to ring, and because of the distinctive ringtone, I knew it was a Snap call. I began smiling shyly as I pushed *accept*. Chaotic's face graced the screen, and his wide smile made me blush harder.

"'Sup, ma?"

"Nothing," I replied, hiding my face.

"Man, I'mma start calling you Shy Girl." He chuckled, making fun of me. "That's crazy, Amor. You've killed niggas, ma, and you scared of me."

"What you mean, 'I've killed niggas'?"

"You think a nigga ain't did his homework on you? I know everything about you, but I'mma say less."

"You don't know shit." I laughed. I hated how much these streets talked. I was trying hard to escape my old life, but it never went unnoticed. "Can I ask you something?"

"Ask."

"What do you want from me?" I asked him on a more serious note.

"Peace," he replied and paused.

I really didn't know what to say because that was what I got from him. I remembered this day he came to see me, and the moment he walked out the door, he stopped, and I could see the intense sigh he let out. It was one of those, *damn, now back to the real world,* kinda sighs. It was like a gift and a curse because I was happy I could bring him peace, but at this point, I wanted more than some desk dates. I wanted this nigga in the worst way, but he was already spoken for.

Chaotic continued to stare into the screen, and it made me smile. We looked each other in the eyes. I had so much to say, but what could I really say?

"Amor," Erica called my name from the front desk, but it was already too late.

Ru was walking in, and he caught me off guard.

I jumped to my feet and ran into the restroom trying not to look obvious to either him or Chaotic.

"What's wrong, ma?"

"Ummm...ummm...he's here."

"Who's there?"

"My...my..."

"Yo' nigga?"

"That's not my..."

"A'ight, go holla at yo' nigga. Yo' ass all in the bathroom hiding and shit." He shook his head and ended the call.

I wanted so badly to call him back, but I remembered Ru was right outside the door. I briefed myself and headed out. I walked back to my desk, and Ru was sitting down.

"What, Ru?"

"I took the baby to my moms."

"Okay. You came all the way up here to tell me that?"

"Man, I just came to see yo' ass." He stood up.

I was able to check him out, and by the way he was

dressed, I could tell he was going out.

"A'ight, I'll see you later. I'm going out tonight."

"Yeah, a'ight." He chuckled and walked out.

I began packing my belongings and headed out right behind him. It was time to turn the fuck up and let my hair down. Literally.

CHAPTER EIGHTEEN

Amor

"Scribble x and O's in my notebook
Checking how my hair and my nails look
I feel myself in a zone
I get nervous when you call..."
-Fantasia

The next morning, I woke up with a pounding ass headache. I had to be at work at ten, and I could barely move. The ringing of my phone was what woke me because I wouldn't have moved. It was Misha calling, asking if she could drop me off to work. Something about her car breaking down. I didn't mind because she didn't have to be at work until eleven, and not to mention, she'd always let me use her car when needed.

I lifted from the bed and began getting dressed. The entire time in the shower, I thought of Chaotic, and he hadn't called me since last night. However, he watched all my stories, and, boy, was I posting. I knew he prolly got the wrong impression because it was Jami and I in a room full of niggas with big clouds of weed and bottles being passed around. Had Ru seen that shit, he would've died, but he didn't even have a Snap.

Once I was done showering, I slid into my clothing. It was easy for me to move around because Heaven was still with her grandmother, and Ru was in the bed passed out. Last night, he, too, had walked in late smelling like a damn drunk Mexican. He climbed into the bed, and I was already drunk, asleep.

Once I was completely done, I headed out the door and headed for Misha's. I sent her a text to let her know I was on the way and to be ready. When I pulled up, I sat out front and waited for her to come out. I started going through Snap, and Chaotic had just posted a video. He was on the freeway with a Rick Ross song playing in his background. *Damn, this nigga fine*, I thought, watching the Snap four more times.

"Damn, bitch." Misha hit the window, scaring the hell out of me.

I got out and let her get into the driver seat. "Damn, did you spray the whole bottle?" I fanned because she had my car lit up with Elly By Frank perfume.

"I know you ain't talking as much Paris Hilton yo' ass be spraying."

"Fuck you."

We laughed, and I lay back in my seat. I looked out the window, into the grey clouds and knew any moment it was gonna start raining.

When we pulled up to my job, I sluggishly got out and

headed inside. This was gonna be a long night because I wasn't getting off until nine p.m. Therefore, wasn't no turning up for me tonight. I couldn't wait to get home and get in my bed.

"Have a good day, friend."

"You too."

I rushed inside. Just as I made it through the door, the rain had begun to come down, and it only made me more tired.

"Ladies, I'm going to the store. Y'all want something?" Brenda from the call center asked.

"Hell yes, a Monster." I reached into my bag and handed her a five dollar bill. I needed a pick-me-up, and fast.

What the bitch want already? I thought, looking at my phone because Misha was calling, and she had pulled off not even ten minutes ago.

"'Sup, Mish?"

"Bitch! Why I'm in McDonald's drive thru, and yo' little boo blocked me in, jumped out, and ran up on the car." She was laughing so hard.

"Who?" I asked because it for damn sure wasn't Ru.

"Girl, Chaotic's crazy ass." Just hearing his name made my heart drop. "He thought it was you. Nigga pulled the door open talking 'bout, 'Where she at?'"

"Oh my God." I blushed so hard. "That boy is crazy." I shook my head and smiled.

"Amor, Dimples!" Erica shouted from the front desk.

Chaotic's car was pulling into a parking stall.

"He's here. I'll call you back."

I hung Misha up just as he was walking in. I tried to act busy as if I didn't see him.

"What's up with you?"

I looked up, and he was standing in front of my desk drenched in water.

"Hey, Canyon." I tried hard to keep a straight face. Inside, I was still laughing at what Misha had told me. I looked at his attire and something was up with the all-black he wore. "What you up to?" I looked at him out of the slit of my eyes.

"I ain't up to shit," he replied, and I could tell he was lying. He began sneezing, and after I told him *bless you* three times, I knew he was getting sick.

"You're getting sick."

"I'm straight. I be back, though. I just came to check in on you."

And just like that, he was gone. I swear this shit was annoying as fuck. It was like he wanted me but didn't want me. I watched as he walked to his car and climbed in. When he pulled out of the stall, he looked through the window, and our eyes met. He held up his phone and signaled that he was gonna call. I nodded my head and began working until I got his call.

These days, it seemed like that was all I did was wait on his call. No matter how much I called myself turning up, I would think about him the entire time. Hell, Ru was leaving room for Chaotic to slide in, and the more Ru and I weren't in each other's presence, the more Chaotic and I talked. ▯

The day had gone by so slow, but my hangover had finally gone away. It was now a quarter to nine, and Misha was still at work. I told her to just go home and how I was okay, so she wouldn't rush. I thought about calling Ru to come get me, but I didn't need him getting any ideas. Instead, I called Chaotic.

"'Sup, Cute Face?"

"Hey. Where are you?"

"Shit, on the highway home."

"Oh, okay."

"Why what's up?"

"I needed a ride home, but it's cool. I don't live far. I could just catch an Uber."

"You sure?"

"Yes, I'm sure."

"A'ight. Well, I'll hit you in a minute."

"Okay."

We hung up, and I began going through my work. I didn't even want to go home just knowing I had to deal with Ru. I tried hard to escape that house, but I guess tonight I didn't have a choice. However, I was gonna stay at work as long as I could.

I continued to get some work done, and before I knew it, another hour had gone by. The entire office was gone, so it was just me. Just as I picked up my phone to call an Uber, Chaotic was at the door looking inside. It was still pouring down raining, so I quickly got up to let him in. He was now bundled up in a black hoodie with a scarf wrapped around his neck.

"You didn't have to come all the way back."

"Man, get yo shit together, so we can go."

"Canyon, you didn't have—"

"Man, you heard what the fuck I said. Now get yo' shit." He walked up on me and pinned me on the desk.

"You always act like you're somebody's daddy."

"And you always act like you like it," he replied lowly, looking me in the eyes.

I didn't say a word because I was too caught up in the moment. This was the closest we'd ever been, and, damn, it felt good. The entire office was so quiet I could hear the sound of us breathing. The only light that shone was the dim light above us, and it beamed right down on him. Although he looked sick as hell, he was still so damn handsome. His lips began moving, and I couldn't make out the shit-talking because my mind was so consumed on kissing him. I couldn't help myself ,so I reached out and pecked his lips.

"I'm sick, ma."

"I don't care," I replied with fire.

He watched me briefly, then let his guards down. His lips touched mine, and we began having a full-blown make out session. This man was kissing me so good my pussy got wet as fuck. I swear I thought my shit was broken because I hadn't gotten wet for a man in a long time. We continued to kiss, and I felt his hand grope my body. Next thing I know, I was opening my legs invitingly. He took one of his fingers into his mouth, slid my panties to the side, and inserted it into me. My head fell back, and a soft moan escaped my lips.

"Damn, I got you wet like this?" He bit into my neck as he continued to toy inside my tunnel. When he slid his finger out of me, I opened my eyes in time to see him insert them into his mouth. He sucked my juices off his finger and looked at me. "Get yo' shit. Let's roll." He turned around to walk out, and I let out a deep sigh.

This nigga had took my body to ecstasy with only a damn finger, then left my ass on *seen*. I had to literally squeeze my legs together to stop the pulsing in between my legs. I went to the other side of my desk and grabbed my things, annoyed. I was so confused and embarrassed that I was scared to go out and face him.

When I made it out, I had to run quickly because the rain was coming down fast. I climbed into his car and took in the smell of his Black Ice air freshener. We pulled away from my job, and I gave him directions to my crib. I knew it was a chance that Ru could come outside, but then again, I knew he wouldn't. Ru didn't check on me. No matter how late I stayed out, that man never called to ask if I was good. He barely asked if I was hungry, and he damn sure didn't inquire about a bill. Ru was all about Ru. Even to the point it surprised me how hands on he was with Heaven.

As we drove toward my home, I looked out the window and pretty much watched the rain. I had so much running through my mind I nearly forgot I was in the car with Chaotic until he asked if I ate. *Damn, my own nigga ain't even asked if I ate,* I thought because Ru knew I wasn't driving today, and he didn't bother to call and ask if I ate lunch. That was where Chaotic was really winning at.

No matter what, he always asked if I had eaten lunch. Not only that; I loved how Chaotic came to see about me. Whether it was five minutes, he still came to see about me. That was all a woman ever wanted was a nigga to make sure she was straight. I hated how another man picked up the slack for a man I had been with for years.

"Why you never call me?" I asked, looking from the rain to Chaotic.

"What you mean? I always call you."

"Yeah, on Snap."

"Open that glove box," he instructed, so I opened it. There was an iPhone that was cracked all over. "I'm bad with phones, ma. I be on my step-daughter shit right now."

"Well, you need to get it fixed."

"I don't really give a fuck about a phone. I don't need the world hunting me down. Really, I only be on social media to talk to yo' ass."

"What about yo' girl? You don't care if it's an emergency?"

"Like I said, I don't need nobody keeping tabs on me."

"Whatever." I put the phone back into the glove box and closed it. "Make a right here, and pull over right there," I told him boldly because we were right across from my home.

"This yo' crib?"

"Yeah."

"What if yo' nigga come out?"

"Then he comes out."

He chuckled followed by a cough.

"Dang, how did you get so sick?"

"Shit, just out in this rain."

"So why didn't you just go in the house when you first felt sick?"

"Because this my weather," he replied, and I knew exactly what he meant.

After doing my homework on him and discovering he was a damn robber and a killer, it didn't surprise me that he loved the rain. I was from the streets, so I knew how this shit went. The hustlers went indoors, and the robbers came out to scope shit. This was the thing I really loved, though. I didn't have to be this hood bitch around him. I got the same results from Chaotic. He wasn't this notorious killer around me. He was always so calm, and to my surprise, a damn gentleman. Therefore, I didn't pry into his street life. Instead, we began talking about things like traveling and agriculture. Before I knew it, we had sat across from my home talking and watching the rain smash into the hood of his car. Just like I said, Ru had never called or come out of the house, which was fine with me.

"As bad as I don't want you to go, you have to get inside," I told Chaotic because he continued to cough. "Thank you for the ride." I smiled and kissed his forehead.

He kissed me one last time and watched me until I made it into my home. I bypassed Ru, who was playing his game, as usual, and the moment I made it to my bedroom, Chaotic was calling me on Snap.

"Dang, you miss me already?"
"Hell yeah. I always miss you when I leave."
"Awww."

I ended up talking to him all the way until he made it home. I told him to call me tomorrow because I didn't know his situation. Just because my nigga didn't care didn't mean it was that easy for him. I knew I was gonna miss him, and with the way he had my pussy creaming today, I would dream about my secret crush.

CHAPTER NINETEEN

Chaotic

"Look, now, I can't promise commitment, but I swear we'll have fun
If you ask, I'll be honest, girl, you not the only one
Just a man on a mission, with my hand on my gun
Couple niggas that hate me, but way more people show love..."
-Nipsey Hussle

Seven days later

After seven whole days of being in the house sick, a nigga was finally feeling better. The entire time I stayed cooped up under the cover, doped up off Promethazine, I watched Amor's multiple Snaps she posted. I had hit her up several times, but not once did she reply. Her last Snap, she was in her car, and because of the time, I knew she was on her way to work.

"Where you going so early?" Mercedes asked, coming into the room.

"I gotta hit the streets. I been in this muthafucka a whole week. Nigga need some money."

"Okay," was her only response.

I knew if I mentioned money, she wouldn't trip, so I used her hunger for dough to my advantage. I grabbed my Cincinnati fitted cap and bent down to kiss her. I patted my pocket for my wallet, then pulled it out to leave it on the dresser. I headed out my crib, and my first stop was T-Mobile to get a phone.

When I pulled up to the phone store, I jumped out and headed inside. I searched the store for Rochell.

"Excuse me, you need to sign in and wait to be called." A T-Mobile associate approached me, but I ignored her.

I spotted Rochell across the room helping a customer, so I made my way over to her. "I need a phone," I interrupted her, making her and the customer look in my direction.

The customer frowned at my rudeness, but I ain't give a fuck.

"Excuse me," Rochell told the lady, then walked over to one of her co-workers. She whispered something to her, and the co-worker headed over to the customer, while Rochell headed back over to me.

"Don't come in my job like that."

"Man, fuck this job."

"Whatever, Canyon. And where you been?"

"I been around."

"You been around? I guess."

"Man, can I get a phone or what? I got shit to do."

"You got yo' ID?"

"Nah," I replied, and she rolled her eyes. "What kind of

phone you want?" she asked, walking over to the phones.

"The latest one. Black."

She rushed to the back to get the phone, so I walked over to the counter to wait. When she came back, she told me the price, so I paid her. She then looked at me as if I was supposed to say something or possibly give her my number, but that wasn't happening. I grabbed the bag from her, said thanks, and walked out the store. I headed to Remy's crib to pick him up, and my next stop was Amor's job because she thought a nigga was playing with her.

When I pulled up to Amor's job, I went in, but she wasn't at her desk. I saw her through the huge picture window of her boss' office, so I took a seat to wait for her. When she finally came into the front office, she rolled her eyes at me and took her seat.

"What's up with you? You don't see my Snaps?" I asked as I laughed her little attitude off.

Instead of replying, she spun her chair around and faced the wall.

This bitch childish as fuck, I thought, watching the back of her.

"For real? So you just spin yo' fucking chair around?" I asked, and, again, she didn't respond. "Man, I'm outta here." I stood to my feet, and that was when I got her attention. I walked out the door, and I could feel her coming behind me.

"So you leaving?" she asked just as I made it to the car.

"Man, I ain't got time for yo' games. I been Snapping you, and you ignoring a nigga, so watch out." I waved her off and opened my door.

"Come here," she called out to me, so I turned around.

Before I knew it, she rushed me against the car and hit me with her can of Monster. I looked at baby girl like she lost her mind. In an instant, I got mad as fuck and just looked at her. We in the middle of a fucking shopping center and this bitch not only rushed me, but threw something at me. It took everything in me not to slide her ass. Instead of knocking her teeth down her throat, I got into my whip angry and embarrassed. I scurried out of her parking lot in a rage and Remy on the side of me quiet.

"Drive." I pulled over, and we switched seats. "Take me to mom's crib, so I can change," I told him, knowing I was gon' be sticky as hell.

On the highway, Remy drove, and I sat on the passenger side lost in my thoughts. I listened to Nipsey Hussle's lyrics, and for some reason, the lyrics got to a nigga.

"Ay, I'm not trippin', back and forth with your nigga
Scared to lose what you got as you lookin' for something different
Me? 'Fly Crippin',' international trippin'
I got my numbers up and now they pay for my statistics..."

It was like my heart was playing tricks on me. I knew I was supposed to be mad at her, but what she had just done was making me have a change of heart.

"Damn, bro, I got two bitches," I looked over to Remy and admitted. This girl had exposed her hand, and it was evident she was falling for me.

"Yeah, she in love with you, my nigga. Bitches don't do shit like this unless they feeling a nigga," Remy replied, but I remained quiet.

My emotions started to get the best of me the more the song played. I had a bitch at home, and Amor had a nigga. I knew in my heart Mercedes wasn't gon' last because, already, she was giving me bad vibes. However, Amor had a family, so I couldn't get emotionally invested. I felt myself already falling for her no matter how much I was in denial. Amor was the bitch I could see my life with. Keep shit real, I really ain't give a fuck about her nigga. I was just trying to dominate these streets. I knew in my heart I was coming back for her, and in the end, it was gon' be us; I just needed time.

Amor

*"Seven whole days
And not a word from you
Seven whole nights
I'm just about through..."*
-Toni Braxton

I walked back into the office with my emotions all over the place. I couldn't believe I acted as such and exposed my true feelings to Chaotic. I couldn't help it. For seven days, I was devastated, and he had my mind all over the place. Nigga had me thinking he ain't want my ass, and that shit was killing me. No call, no text, no Snap, nothing. Then he had the nerve to walk into my job like shit cool.

After the day in the office when he played with my pussy, that shit only added to my feelings. Then, the way we vibed in front of my house, in the rain, I thought we were going some-where. Silly me. So for seven whole muthafucking days, my en-ergy was off, and I hated the nigga. I hated when my emotions were played with. I mean, I understood he was sick, but, damn. He could've at least texted.

"You like him."

I looked up, and Jami was staring at me. I remained quiet, and she was still watching me out the slits of her eyes.

Damn, I really exposed myself, I thought because of the way she was saying it. "Fuck him," I finally spoke right when my phone went off. I knew it was him, so I ignored it, too embarrassed to answer.

"So what's up with your hubby?" she asked, changing the subject from Chaotic to Ru.

The question caught me off guard because she hadn't been here to know right now I wasn't fucking with Ru. The other night when we went to the studio, I didn't get a chance to catch her up on everything because it was a room full of people.

"I don't know, Jami. I'm just ready to give up on that whole relationship. It's like the thrill is gone, you know?"

"Yep. It be like that. So are you ready to throw it away for him?" she asked, referring to Chaotic.

I paused momentarily, then turned in my chair to face her. "Yeah and no. He got a bitch, first and foremost. I like him, though. He's like a knight in shining armor if you know what I mean." She nodded her head *yes,* so I continued. "It's like, when the world is on my shoulders, he's right on time. That man be busy with his own life, but no matter what, he comes to see about me. The way Ru is supposed to make me feel, Chaotic picks up the slack. However, one minute, he's into me, then he disappears, so that shit be having me confused. I want him to just leave me the fuck alone at times, but in my heart, I want him in my space. I don't know, man. This shit weird as fuck." I sighed, not knowing how to explain the situation with us.

I know I was not supposed to be falling for this nigga, but how could I not? He was everything I wanted, but he was forbidden.

A few hours later

I saw the tail end of Chaotic's car, so I got up from my desk and headed out before he came in. He pulled into the empty space, and when he didn't get out, I took it upon myself to get in. I was so nervous my palms began to sweat, but I was ready for him to curse my ass out. The car was silent for a brief moment until he decided to speak.

"What's yo' problem?"

"I don't have a problem."

"Shit, you got something." He sat back in his seat, and I noticed he had changed clothes.

I began to bite into my bottom lip trying to figure out what to say. I wanted to be real with him, but I was too afraid to admit my true feelings.

"Seven fucking days, Canyon?"

"Amor, I was sick, ma."

"I don't care. You could've called, texted, something."

"I was really fucked up. I couldn't even move. That whole time I was in bed off meds."

"I understand, but you could've still called. I felt like you just didn't want me."

"Man, stop thinking like that. I want you more than you know, but I can't have you."

"Why, 'cause yo' bitch?"

"Nah, because yo' nigga." He looked at me seriously.

When I didn't speak, he shook his head, and I could see the frustration on his face. I wanted so badly to tell him Ru and I weren't what he thought, but it wouldn't matter because he was still spoken for.

"You belong to *me,* ma. Never forget that." He started his engine, so I knew what that meant.

I opened the door, but before I climbed out, he grabbed my

arm.

"Let me see yo' phone."

I handed him my cell. He began punching numbers in it, then the phone sitting on his lap rang. He then punched something else into my phone and handed it back.

"Now gimme kiss."

I reached over and puckered my lips. His nice, full lips pressed against mine, and I melted. I closed my eyes to savor the moment, and when I opened them, he was looking dead at me. I held his gaze for a brief moment until the frustration of not being able to have him kicked in. I got out of his car and watched him until he pulled out of the lot. Fuck, I wanted that man in the worst way, but that was wishful thinking.

CHAPTER TWENTY

Amor

"No One Else Can Do What You Do For Me
Take Me Away From The Pain
I Feel Inside
It's Going To Be Alright, It Will Be Ok
If We Try And Take Our Time Please Baby Take Your Time
And We'll Grow Trust I Know..."
- Keyshia Cole

After weeks of rainfall, the air was fresh, and the sun began to shine brightly. It was so beautiful outside that I was dressed bright and early, ready to hit the hood. Misha was already on her way, and Rawdy was already hanging out. I went to the safe that I kept in my closet and pulled a band for food and liquor. I then grabbed my Burberry handbag that matched my glasses and belt and headed for the door. I was looking good and feeling great thanks to my secret boo.

Since the day I threw the Monster on him, we had been kicking it more. Nothing had moved forward between us, but I could feel the difference. He finally had a phone, so we talked more outside of Snapchat. The day he took my phone, he had stored himself as *Ryda* and stored me as *Gutta Baby* in his. Although we had begun vibing more, I still felt lonely. There was an emptiness inside of me from the space between Ru and I, and Chaotic not being mine officially. He didn't give me a title, but he did call me his Gutta Baby, and it was cute.

As I walked through the living room, I tried to move fast past Ru. He was on his game, and I couldn't help but stop because Heaven was lying peacefully in her chair next to him. I wanted so badly to just stay home and be with my child, but I was still running from my problems. I used my emptiness to run the streets, and right now, it was working. A part of me was open to dating someone because the truth remained, Chaotic had a girl. Ru hadn't stepped up to the plate and sat me down to make amends. So I felt free to do as I pleased.

"Like A Candy, To An Apple
Oh, We Go Together
You're So Sweet On Me
I Can Say That I Do Believe
This Is Destiny
It Keeps Calling Me..."

I sang to the lyrics of Aaliyah's "It's Whatever" as I pulled up to the hood. My girls were already here, but because my part to the song was coming up, I stayed in the car listening. *"Whatever Is Whatever, It's Whatever, It's Your World, I Put That On Everything."* I smiled at the part because it made me think of my Ryda.

I swear, at this point in my life, it was whatever he wanted it to be. All he had to do was say the word, and I would pack my shit and go. I already had plans to leave Ru the house and kid. I didn't wanna seem unfit because I loved my daughter to death, but he wanted the baby. Therefore, I knew he wouldn't just let me fully move on with his child.

And anyway, why did the man always get to leave? Why couldn't we pack our shit and go? I would leave him the house and a car or two and start completely over.

"Bitches in love and shit." Misha snatched my car door open laughing.

I smiled hard because she already knew what was up. Misha was the one I could talk to about Chaotic. Rawdy, on the other hand, wasn't having that shit. She hated them niggas, and believe it or not, she caught a body or two over there.

"Ugh, this nigga." I rolled my eyes at the homie, Boss.

He was one of those niggas who ran his mouth too much, and anything he saw me doing, he would report to Ru. After the night at the club, I noticed he'd been moving funny. Ru knew my every move, and I knew it was him. Nigga had his nerve, tho', because he knew everything Ru did and ain't report shit to me. Ru and I were both his girl, so I felt he should've just stayed out of it; just as Rawdy did. Rawdy was a nigga for real. She knew everything Ru did, but she minded her business.

"Fuck him." Misha did the same thing I had done and rolled her eyes. She already knew what was up, but fuck him. "I got a bottle. You wanna start drinking?"

"I don't care. Let me pull into the yard, so I could play the music."

I got back into my car and pulled inside the gate. I went to my playlist and the first song I played was EST Gee "5500 Degrees." I turned the music up to the max and had the entire yard rattling. Misha began to pour our drinks, then walked over to the dice game to give Rawdy a cup.

Misha and I leaned on my ride and began gossiping about our sex lives. We ain't believe in hood gossip because there was nothing interesting to us in the hood or around the world for that matter. That was one thing I never did; gossip. Therefore, my name wasn't dragged in *he say, she say.*

I began popping my ass to Lil Baby's "All In" while I held the bottle in the air.

"Damn," I cursed because my phone began ringing right when my part was coming up. I bent down into the car to get it and hesitated when I saw it was Chaotic.

"Hello?"

"'Sup, ma? Where you at?"

"I'm...I'm at home."

"Man, you a muthafucking lie! I'm looking dead at you dancing, holding a fucking bottle in yo' hand!" he barked, and I could tell he was aggy because I tried to lie.

I began looking around to see where was he, and I knew it had to be him sitting in the middle of the street behind some dark ass tints. My heart began pounding because he sat there not giving two fucks about traffic, nor the homies. All I needed was one of these niggas to see him, and all hell would break loose.

"Bitch," I alerted Misha, and she quickly looked at me. "That's him," I told her nervous as hell.

"Go." She grabbed the bottle from me, and even she looked scared.

I quickly walked out to the middle of the street, and he made a U-turn. I opened the passenger door and climbed inside.

"Pull off," I told him in fear. The nigga looked at me like I was crazy and sat right here. "Pull off, Canyon."

"Man, I ain't pulling off shit. You think I'm scared of these niggas? Amor, my daddy died fa' this shit." He looked at me with an evil glare.

I didn't know what he meant about 'his father dying for this shit,' but I needed him to pull off. I was looking out the window, and I saw Boss looking in our direction. The windows were deep black, so they couldn't see inside; however, they knew I had jumped in.

"Please, Canyon," I pleaded, and he pulled off slowly.

When we made it to the corner, I sighed deeply because this was all I needed. One, he was an enemy, and two, it was disrespect to Ru.

"Where the fuck yo' nigga at?" he asked without looking in my direction.

"Home."

"So the nigga just let you do what the fuck you want?" Again, he shook his head.

"No."

"No, my ass. You hanging out and shit, ma. Hennessy bottles in yo' fucking hand."

"I'm grown, Chaotic," I replied sarcastically.

"Man, shut yo' dumb ass up. Where yo pistol?"

"In my car." I matched his energy.

He didn't say another word. Instead, he looked straight ahead and continued to drive. The car fell silent, and I knew then he was mad. I looked out the window, not knowing what else to say.

"You eat?" he asked, pulling my attention in his direction.

"No," I replied nervously because I knew he would say something about me drinking on an empty stomach. To my surprise, he didn't say nothing. "So what you mean about, 'yo' pops died for this shit'?" I asked, changing the subject.

"My pops a general in yo' hood. Skoob. Got killed when I was, like, four."

"Big Skoob yo' pops?" I asked shocked.

Big Skoob was my big homie who was murdered by some enemies years ago. I was too young when it happened, but growing up, my homies spoke highly of him. Pretty much everyone had Skoob's name tatted, and every year for hood day, the homies would wear shirts with his name and picture on them.

"Yep. First nigga in yo' hood to get killed by a Crip."

"Damn, I didn't know that was yo' dad."

Again, the car fell silent, and we were pulling into Taco Lady's parking lot. I looked at Chaotic as if he was crazy because this place was surrounded by his enemies. My hood, and a couple more blood hoods, were the surrounding sets. I watched him hard, but I didn't wanna say shit. He jumped out the car as if it was nothing, but before he walked off, he looked down at me. ▢

"One day, you gon' learn who the fuck I am." He closed the door and went to the window to order our food.

I sat back in my seat nervously because this nigga was crazy. I had always heard about this man, and now I was seeing it firsthand.

While I was waiting on Chaotic to get the food, I sent Misha a text to pick me up. I knew by the time the food was ready, she'd be coming. I didn't wanna take the chance of him dropping me back on the block. When I looked up to make sure Chaotic was straight, I couldn't help but admire his gangsta. He was standing there as if he didn't have a care in the world. He wore a cold mean-mug, and it made me wonder what was going through his head. I swear this nigga was oppressive. It was like something was always weighing heavy on his mind.

Just as he was walking back over with our burritos, Misha was turning into the lot. *Thank God*, I thought, watching my car pull in.

"Aye, we gotta pick Heaven up, bitch!" she yelled out the window to play it off.

"Okay, here I come," I replied and held up one finger to let her know give me a second. "I gotta get my baby." I then looked at Chaotic.

He reached into the bag and handed me my food.

"Thank you." I puckered my lips, so he'd give me a kiss.

He reached over and kissed my lips. "Yeah, let me roll back by and you over there." He started his engine, so I climbed out.

"Okay, daddy," I shot sarcastically into his car, and he

chuckled.

"I'm 'bout to call yo ass too." He rolled the window up before I could reply.

I headed over to the car and climbed in.

"Bitch, that nigga crazy as hell."

Misha and I watched as he pulled out the lot.

"Crazy ain't the word." I sat back in my seat with all types of things running through my mind. I was feeling the fuck out this nigga, and by the days, shit was getting deeper.

"The homies were asking who you left with. I ain't know what to say, so I told them to mind their business. Boss' nosey ass was looking hard too. Amor, what you gon' do with this nigga because, baby, he ain't playing with you. He bold as fuck, but y'all gotta get that shit under control. If Ru finds out this nigga pulling up like that, shit gon' get wild."

"I already know, Mish. Shit, he crazy. I can't tell him shit. And trip this. His dad is Big Skoob."

"Big Skoob, RIP?"

"Yep."

"Damn, that's crazy." She had the same reaction I did. "Yeah, friend, you gotta figure your life out. If you gon' fuck with him, then leave Ru completely alone. Now I don't know how the homies gonna take it, but that's the first step." She went on and on, but my mind was elsewhere.

I knew everything she was saying was true, but it was complicated. Chaotic had a bitch; period. Therefore, I couldn't just decide that easily. All I knew was, I was falling deep by the days. I was too afraid to admit that someone was gonna get hurt by this love scandal. Physically or emotionally, and I felt it coming.

CHAPTER TWENTY ONE

Chaotic

"Ya never had a father or a family, but I'll be there
No need to fear so much insanity
And through the years
I know ya gave me your heart and plus
When I am dirt broke and fucked up you'll still love me..."
-Tupac

I walked into the bedroom to see if Mercedes was dressed and ready to roll. I didn't know if my mind was playing tricks on me, but the bitch dropped her phone fast. Ignoring it, I continued into the restroom to grab my phone and wallet.

Mercedes stood to her feet, and the look on her face was

evident she had an attitude.

"What's up with you? Fix yo' face before we leave this house."

"Nigga, fix the bullshit you be doing," she shot, shocking the fuck outta me.

"What bullshit I be doing?" I asked, followed by a chuckle.

"It ain't funny. You tagging bitches, and I noticed you ignore everyone in your comments except this one bitch." She lifted her phone to show me.

"Man, that's my pops little homegirl. Ain't shit going on with that girl."

"Delete her."

"Delete her? I ain't deleting that girl."

I shook my head thinking about Ashley. This was the same bullshit as before. I didn't know why, but these girls were threatened by Amor. I mean, shit, she was bad and had her shit together, so it was understood why everyone was so pressured by her.

"Yeah, I bet." She rolled her eyes and stormed into the front room.

I followed behind her, and she was walking out the door. I grabbed the keys from the counter and headed out.

The car ride to the club was silent, and I knew this shit was gonna fuck my night up. Mercedes sat on the passenger side of me with her lips poked out, looking out the window. I really didn't give two fucks about her attitude, so I turned on my Tee Grizzley CD and vibed out to the music.

When we pulled up, I parked my whip in the front and tipped the valet to keep it right there. Mercedes took her time getting out, and that shit annoyed me more. I walked ahead of her to holla at security. Already knowing what's up, I slid him a rack on the low, and he nodded his head. I headed inside to find my brother and homies, and when I looked back, Cedes was still slow-dragging. Tonight was my little brother's birthday, so we were going up in VIP with strippers and bottles. I wasn't 'bout to let this bitch fuck my night up, so I was gonna ignore her.

When we made it inside the club, the place was packed, and it looked like a cool environment. I was hoping it would be a cool crowd because I didn't wanna have to air this place out. This was one reason I hated partying because all kinds of niggas from everywhere would be in the facility. This club had just opened and was the most talked about club in the city, but to my surprise, wasn't any familiar faces. Another thing, I wondered how many niggas did the security let in with their guns. I paid him a grand, and it was just that easy.

"Broooo!" my lil brother yelled out the moment he spotted me. "'Sup, Cedes?" he spoke half interested.

He really wasn't feeling her, but on the strength of me, he dealt with her. The first time he met her, he pulled me to the side and said it was something about her he didn't like. He went on to tell me about a couple niggas she fucked with, but that was her business. I wasn't saying I didn't pay attention to what he was saying, but this was my bitch, and everyone had to deal with it.

"Happy birthday," she told him and took a seat.

"Bigggg!" Lady Chaotic screamed out and ran over to hug me.

I couldn't help but laugh because she had on a little ass dress with a big ass purse that told me she had a big ass gun inside. This girl was more gangsta than a lot of niggas, and I could trust her with my life. Lady and I had not only laid shit down together, but we even caught a couple bodies together.

"'Sup, sis?" I wrapped my arm around her and pulled her to the side. "Aye, keep her company for me." I nodded over to Mercedes.

Lady looked at her, then back to me. I knew she wouldn't tell me no, but I could also see she ain't really wanna be bothered. Lady didn't care for Mercedes either, and I knew it was because of her cousin, Tuck. My lady was just like me when it came to these niggas. She ain't trust shit and always told me watch that nigga. I had introduced them a couple months ago, but, of course, Cedes was kinda standoffish.

"Ugh, okay," she replied and walked over to where Cedes sat.

I watched as she picked up a bottle of liquor and began pouring them a drink. I used this to move around the club and scope out the scene. Whoever the owner was had bread because the club was nice. Being that it was the grand opening, I knew he would be somewhere around, and if he was, he would be getting the same treatment as Raphael.

"Excuse me, sexy." I stopped the most gullible-looking waitress who crossed my path.

"Hey." She smiled wide.

I couldn't help but expose my dimples. Bitch prolly thought I was smiling at her, but I was really tripping off the fact of how easy these hoes were.

"Who's the owner of this place? I'm trying to find out about a party for Jason Stone, quarterback from the NFL," I lied, making up some shit.

At just the mention of the NFL, the bitch got thirsty.

"Oh, he's in his office. William, but you can't go back there."

"I understand. By any chance, what kinda car does he drive? I'll holla at him on his way out."

"The silver Porsche 911."

"A'ight. Make sure you come to the VIP, so I can see yo' sexy ass again."

"Okay." She giggled and rushed off holding a tray with drinks on it.

I went outside to search for the car she said William drove, and after searching the front, I found the car in the rear lot parked off to the side by itself. I searched the area for any hidden cameras, and when I didn't see any, I bent down to place the tracker underneath the car. *This shit too easy*, I thought, heading back inside.

When I made it back up to the VIP, it was now time to have a drink and relax. I took a seat next to Mercedes and poured me a drink. I reached over and kissed her cheek, so she could fix her attitude. When she looked up at me, she tried hard to have an attitude, but she couldn't resist my smile. She faintly smiled back, and I knew then I had her. The liquor definitely kicked in because she had begun to loosen up. She was rapping along to the City Girls, and Lady was on the side of her hyping her up. When I noticed her drink nearly gone, I poured her another cup.

"Aye, bro, check it out one time." My brother called me over.

I got up from my seat and headed over to him.

"There go ol' girl." He nodded, and my eyes followed in that direction.

I watched as Amor and her friends were in some niggas' faces, and she was smiling too hard. The nigga she was talking to had just left from the VIP, a few booths down from us, so when he grabbed her hand, I knew where he was leading her to.

I watched as Amor came up the steps trailing behind the nigga. The moment she reached the top of the stairs, our eyes met, and she froze. She looked at me, then her eyes fell onto Mercedes. A frown slid across her face, and she mugged Cedes. She then rolled her eyes and followed the crowd into the section. I watched her in her little ass dress, and this really pissed me off.

"This bitch gon' make me fuck her up," I thought out loud, and my brother heard me.

"Chill, fool, yo' girl here." He tried to reason with me, but I ain't give a fuck.

In my eyes, Amor was my future, and Mercedes was something to do for the moment. Therefore, her being here and on some ratchet ass shit wasn't sitting well with me.

I walked over and took my original seat, and just my luck, one of them hoe ass Megan Thee Stallion songs came on. Cedes was now good and drunk, so she got up from her seat and started dancing on my lap. I snuck a peek over at Amor, and, again, our eyes met. I could tell by the look on her face she wanted so bad to trip, but her homegirl whispered something in her ear that got her attention.

Whatever she said made her jump to her feet and start popping her ass. I didn't sweat it. I took a swig from the bottle as Cedes continued to pop her thick ass on my dick. When I glanced in Amor's direction again, one of the niggas had her bent over as she bounced her ass on him. I tried to laugh it off, but fuck that; I lost it.

"Watch out," I told Cedes, and she lifted up off me.

I stormed over to where Amor was, and her homegirl nudged her arm. By the time she looked up, I was already standing in front of her. She pursed her lips and crossed one arm over the other.

"Come here, ma," I told her in my most calmest voice.

She looked at me as if she was gonna object, but after learning the type of nigga I was, she knew not to play with me. She walked over to me and looked me in the eyes.

"What Chaotic?"

"So this what you doing?"

"I'm doing what you doing. Man, go back over there with yo' bitch before I cause a scene and expose yo' dumb ass." She tried to be tough.

I laughed it off, but the shit only made me madder. "On my daddy, you and yo' friends got ten minutes to finish having fun with these niggas. If I gotta come back over here..." I took her hand and put it on the butt of my pistol.

I walked away from her, and there was nothing left to be said. When I got back over to Mercedes, she sat with her arms folded. This told me she knew exactly who Amor was. Like I said before, I ain't give a fuck. I grabbed the bottle and guzzled some down as I counted in my head. This bitch had about seven more minutes before bullets started flying. I sat back and pulled out my phone. I could feel Cedes watching me, but I ignored her.

Me: *Four mins!*

I slid my phone back into my pocket and finished my drink.

"Why we leaving?" I heard a female's voice.

"Because my daddy said I gotta go." I heard Amor reply sarcastically.

I looked up just in time to see her walk by, and she rolled her eyes. I watched her until she was out the door, and I could still feel Cedes watching me.

"Yo' little bitch left."

"That ain't my bitch. And I know; I made her leave," I replied since she wanted to be funny.

She rolled her eyes but didn't say shit else. She began texting on her phone like I was supposed to be mad. I grabbed another bottle from the ice bucket, sat back, and was gonna finish enjoying the night with my bro.

CHAPTER TWENTY TWO

Amor

"I think I'm falling for somebody else and I can't control myself
It's like some kind of hex on me
Controlling who I love and how I speak..."
-Ashanti

After a long bullshit night in the club, I brought my drunk ass home. Because Chaotic made me leave, it was still kinda early, and a part of me wanted to stay out with Misha. However, I decided to just go home, so I could curl up with my baby. When I walked into my crib, the house was dark, and Ru wasn't in his normal spot. Assuming they were gone, I

143

headed to my room. When I cut on the lights, I had to take a step back astonishingly. There were rose petals scattered out over the floor, and they led to the bed. On the bed was a stuffed animal with flowers and a bottle of Hennessy beside it. Had this been another lifetime, I probably would have been excited. Instead, I rolled my eyes and stepped right over the petals.

Ru was lying in the bed, and I knew he had to be awake because of all the noise I was making. I guess he expected for me to be excited, but fuck him. My night was ruined. This nigga, Chaotic, had me in my feelings; therefore, all I wanted to do was sleep. The nerve of the nigga sending me home when he had his bitch right there. Not only that, but he hadn't called once. The way I was feeling had me on my *fuck him* tip. It wasn't because I was mad he made me leave; it was because I wasn't used to no shit like this.

This nigga was doing something to me I couldn't explain. It was like he had some sort of power over me. I didn't know why, but I was submissive to him effortlessly. I've never in my life been submissive to a nigga, not even Ru. No man in life ran my program, and now here it was, a nigga I barely knew, hadn't been in my life but a few months, and wasn't even mines came in and changed shit up. That was the scary part.

"Ru, scoot over." I pouted as I kicked off my shoes.

I took off my clothing and didn't bother taking a shower. I knew I smelled like niggas, and I didn't give a fuck. He rolled over and looked at me, so I took it upon myself to thank him.

"Thanks for the Hennessy." I chuckled because he was a straight joke.

This was something I was used to. Whenever he fucked up, he would buy me flowers and Hennessy. Nope, shit wasn't gonna work this time.

When I got in the bed, my phone began to ring. My heart dropped hearing the Aaliyah "It's Whatever" ringtone I had stored Chaotic under. Ru was still looking at me, so I knew I had to play it off.

"I made it in, bitch," I spoke into the phone after sending the call to voicemail. I took this as my chance to power it off because I knew he would call back. I was over Ru's ass, and I was now over Chaotic. *The hell with both these niggas.* I fluffed my pillow, frustrated, and finally lay my ass down. I lay still, deep in my thoughts as my head spun. Before I knew it, I opened my eyes, and the sun was peeking through the blinds.

"Amor, telephone," Ru said as soon as I was awake.

"Who is it?"

"It's yo' job," he replied and handed me the phone.

"Hello?"

"Good morning, Amor. Can you come in for four hours? We're packed today, and Jami is the only one here."

"Okay, let me get up," I told my boss and disconnected the line. I handed Ru back his phone and lifted from the bed to start getting ready.

After taking a long, hot shower, I climbed out and slid into my clothes. Because it was a Sunday, my boss didn't mind us being comfy. However, because it was packed, so I still made sure I looked presentable. Once I was done, I went into Heaven's room, and she wasn't there.

"Ru, where's my baby!" I yelled into the next room.

"She's with my mom. They going to Disneyland today."

"Oh, okay," I replied and quickly walked out.

Ru thought he was so slick. He bought me Hennessy and sent my baby away. He definitely thought he was getting my pussy.

"I'm out, Ru."

"Mhmm," he replied with an attitude that I ignored.

I headed out the door fast because I heard an argument in his voice ready to happen.

❤️🞏🞏🞏

"**M**ay I help you?" I jumped up from my desk to help a customer. Jami was busy with a customer, and Erica was off today, so we had to work the front.

"Yeah, I'm here to file."

"Okay, fill this out." I handed the gentleman the clipboard and an ink pen.

"Good looking." He smiled flirtatiously, and I couldn't help but smile back.

He was actually a bit cute with an older demeanor. He wasn't no Chaotic, but he was definitely handsome. He had a perfect goatee, locs that hung past his shoulders, and a nice ass body that I could see through his white-tee.

"Step over here when you done," I informed him and headed back over to my desk.

"You know him?" Jami asked, eyeing the nigga I had just helped.

"No."

"He looks hella familiar. He's cute." She smiled, checking him out from head to toe.

Moments later, the guy walked over and handed me the clipboard. He took a seat, and I began entering his data into the system.

"Excuse me, do you be at the studio on eighty-ninth?" Jami asked from her desk.

"Money?" he asked, and she nodded. "Yeah, that's my cousin."

"The studio we were at a couple weeks ago?" I asked Jami, and she nodded. I focused on the guy, then looked down at his paper and read the name, Donovan. "Where you from, Donovan?" I asked more on an unprofessional note. I didn't normally do this, but knowing Money and hanging out at the studio, he had to be affiliated.

"I'm from Piru." He chuckled, already knowing what I meant. By the tattoos on my body, and the few on my face that I couldn't hide, I guess he figured I was from the streets.

"Okay, me too." I smiled, and after that we began to chat comfortably.

He leaned in his chair and loosened up. From time to time, Jami joined in on the conversation, and we all talked as if we had been knowing each other for years.

"Put yo' number in my phone." He slid his phone across my desk, and I smiled.

I normally didn't give niggas my number because of Ru, but with the way things were going, now why not? I put my number in his phone, and soon as I slid it back to him, I heard Jami's voice.

"Uhh-ohhh."

I looked up, and Chaotic was walking into the office.

"Here, sign right here, here, here, and here." I slid Donovan's 1040 across the table and jumped to my feet. "Give me one minute," I told Donovan as Chaotic looked him up and down.

"What, Canyon?" I asked the moment we were outdoors.

"Who the fuck is that?"

"A client."

"So why the fuck you explaining yo' self to him?"

"He's just a client. I don't know him." I rolled my eyes.

"Yeah, a'ight."

"Is that what you came here for? Just to talk shit and clock what the fuck I'm doing?"

"Man, fuck you."

"Fuck you too."

He walked off toward his car.

I swear I couldn't stand this nigga. I stormed back into my office because this nigga had just taken my energy.

"My bad, Donovan."

"Don B."

"Excuse me, Don B."

"Nah, you good." He chuckled and retrieved his paperwork from the desk. "I'mma hit you up."

"Okay, you do that." I blushed, and he headed out.

"What yo' boyfriend talking 'bout?" Jami asked, referring to Chaotic.

"That ain't my boyfriend. Fuck him."

"Yeah, that's what yo' mouth says." She laughed, but I ain't see shit funny. "Anyway, what's up? Let's hit the streets tonight. I'll call to see if they turning up at the studio."

"I'm down," I replied and looked over at the clock.

It was already time to go, but Jami and I stayed behind talking. We had Ashanti's Pandora playing low in the overhead speakers, and she even had a pint of Remy Martin in the car. We poured ourselves a cup and locked the doors. We were officially closed and about to have us a sip before turning up later.

CHAPTER TWENTY THREE

Chaotic

*"Top down, right here is where she wanna be
As my goals unfold right in front of me..."*
-Rick Ross

"Ohhh, shitttt!"

Mercedes screamed out as I pounded inside of her. I had been fucking her for nearly an hour, and for some reason, I couldn't nut.

"Turn over," I told her, and she quickly turned on all fours. I lifted her ass in the air and slid back inside of her. I closed my eyes and began to imagine it was Amor. I was still pissed off at baby girl since I left her job, so I was gonna take it out on Cedes' pussy.

"Oh, my! Shittttt, baby, you killing... Aghhhhh, baby, you... You killing me!"

"Man, take this dick, and shut up!" I continued fucking her until sweat began to pour from my body. When I finally felt the nut build up, I forcefully squeezed her ass. "Grhhhhhhhh!" I howled until I emptied every drop into her.

Instead of pulling out, I fell on top of her and rolled her to her side so my dick wouldn't come out. I pulled her close to me, and I could feel her body still shaking. She was still trying to catch her breath while I was still envisioning Amor lying in my arms.

"Love you."

I opened my eyes to Mercedes' voice. I really ain't know what to say, but it was only right I replied.

"Love you too." The room fell silent until she dropped a bomb on me.

"Canyon, I'm pregnant."

Again, my eyes shot open, and I had become alert. I lifted up from the bed, and instead of replying, I slid into my clothes, grabbed my keys, and headed out the house.

When I got in my whip, my phone began going off, but I let it go to voicemail. I held it in my hand as I watched Cedes call over and over. I didn't know why, but right now, I ain't have shit to say to her. I needed to get my mind right, and the only way to do that was to see *her.*

Me: *Way?*

Seven minutes later.

Gutta Baby: *I'm out. Why, what's up?*
Me: *I need to see you. I'm not asking you, I'm telling you.*

Gutta Baby: 🔲 *4901 E 89th Street.*
Me: *Omw .*

I clicked on the address and followed my GPS to the location. It said I would be there in forty-five minutes, but the way I was driving I knew it would be sooner. I turned my music up and tried hard to get Cedes off my mind. I knew I was wrong for the way I left, but I had to leave before I said some shit I'd regret. I could hear it in her voice she was scared to tell me she was pregnant, but I could also draw out the excitement, and that was what fucked me up. I wasn't ready for another baby. This wasn't part of the plan, so I wasn't gonna sit back and act like I was happy.

"Would have came back for you, I just needed time
To what I had to do, caught in the life
I can't let it go, whether that's right I will never know
But here goes nothing..."

Pulling up to the address Amor gave me, I let the lyrics to "Aston Martin Music" soothe me. I felt this song, and it was something 'bout the words that fit perfectly how I felt. I definitely would come back for Amor, but right now, I needed time. I was caught up in the life, and the streets was all I knew at the moment. Don't get me wrong, I knew how to be a good nigga, but I also needed to put myself in a position that would help me sit down. The few licks I hit had me sitting on a couple hunnid bands, but I needed more. When the time came, it would be Amor who I was gonna wife. I just needed her to have patience. I had plans to spoil baby girl, and that was my mission.

Me: *I'm outside.*
Gutta Baby: *Here I come.*

I dropped my phone because now that I was with my Gutta Baby, it was useless. Cedes was texting me, but not once did I open the thread. I watched as Amor emerged from the house, and my face instantly frowned. She was looking good as fuck in her little ass dress. I didn't mind a woman dressing as such, but only when she was with me.

"Why you outside so late?" Amor asked, getting in my whip.

"Whose house is this?" I ignored her question and asked.

"It's a studio."

"Studio full of niggas." I snarled and turned my music up. I headed for the highway and hit repeat on the song.

As we drove the highway, the air seeped in, and the coast was clear. I told Amor hand me the bottle of Hennessy on the floor, then took a swig. I then poured her a cup as I drank out the bottle. The moment I put the cork back in and sat the bottle down, she took my hand into hers and squeezed it tight. I didn't know why, but this did something to me. I squeezed hers back to let her know we were on the same page, and it felt good having her in my presence.

Thirty minutes later, we were pulling up to the beach, so we could talk. I wanted to get some shit off my chest. I just hoped she wouldn't trip. I needed her as a friend right now, and not my bitch, so I was gonna open up.

❤️🖤🖤🖤

"Why you so quiet? What's on your mind?"

"All types of shit, ma."

"I can tell."

"How's that?"

"Well, for one, Canyon, you don't smoke weed, and you hitting that blunt like it's the last high on earth. Second, you always talking shit, and since I've been with you, you've been quiet."

"Girl, you don't know me." I chuckled and took another hit from the blunt.

I looked out into the water and watched the waves crash against shore. Amor and I ended up on the beach because, like I said, I needed to clear my head. After every lick, this was the place I'd come to for peace. I never let women stress me out, so I never came for that.

"So what's wrong?" Amor fell down into the sand and wrapped her arm through mines.

"She pregnant," I finally admitted in a low tone.

I dropped my head and waited for whatever sarcastic shit Amor had to say. However, she didn't say a word. Instead, she got quiet and stood up to her bare feet. I watched her as she walked closer into the ocean, and it was like she went into a daze. I continued to watch her momentarily until I decided to get up and join her. I walked over to where she stood, not caring that my shoes and the cuffs of my pants were getting wet. I wrapped my arms around the small of her waist, but she rejected my embrace and spun around.

"I don't want you to have a baby." Her voice cracked as she turned to hide her face.

I forcefully made her look at me, and I could see she was hurt. A few strands of her hair blew from the breeze, and she looked me dead in my eyes. It was something about the look she was giving me that helped make up my mind. I didn't bother to tell her because one thing I never did was speak about my relationship. I couldn't even just say me because Amor never spoke on hers either. When we were together, we'd forget about everything going on in our lives. It was like we were both each other's calm, so shit outside of us didn't exist. Our time spent with one another wasn't taken for granted, so we wouldn't dare ruin it speaking on the next nigga or bitch.

I knew Amor prolly thought differently, but I wasn't in love with Cedes. I mean, I took a liking to her and her daughter but wasn't no love there. Our relationship was pretty much rushed, and we never got to learn things about one another. The way things were looking lately, I knew it was a matter of time we would split.

"What's my favorite soda?" I asked, knowing it prolly sounded dumb, but I needed to hear her say it.

"Dr. Pepper, why?" she replied, and I smiled on the inside.

This told me she paid attention to the little things. Just like when she asked why was I out so late. That also let me know she paid attention to the way I ran my program. One thing about me, I made sure to always be in by the time that sun went down. Out of respect for my relationship because it wasn't shit outside at night but bitches and trouble.

"I love you, ma," I spoke sincerely, and I meant it.

"I love you too," she replied, and I could tell she ain't want to.

I didn't know why, but for some reason, her love felt genuine. It was like her words touched a nigga's soul, and her actions always spoke volumes. I knew Amor loved me, and hearing her say it, at a time like this, really helped me make up my mind. I wasn't having that baby, and as bad as I didn't wanna hurt Cedes, I had to. I ain't see no future with her, and a baby would bond us together for a lifetime.

"Canyon, I love you." She spoke again as if I didn't hear her the first time.

I looked at her briefly for any signs of inconstancy, and when I didn't see any, I kissed the top of her forehead. "I know."

CHAPTER TWENTY FOUR

Amor

*"I don't wanna rain on this parade
But I'm starting to question the love that was made
I'm not looking for just an affair
Wanna love that is based on truth not just dare…"*
-Brownstone

One month later

Super Bowl Sunday

"Here you go in yo' damn Raiders."

"Don't hate."

"I ain't hating. My team playing." Jami did a little dance and spun in her one-piece Patriots outfit.

I playfully rolled my eyes because, although my team wasn't playing in the bowl, I was still repping. I wore a custom black bodycon Raiders dress with a pair of black ankle boots. The Patriots were playing the Falcons, and Jami was a diehard Pat, so she went all out on her fit. We were about to hit a Super Bowl party given by Don B.

Since that day at the office, we had kept in contact. He even came to the studio a few times to see me. Don B was mad cool, but the way I was caught up over Chaotic, I didn't put effort into moving past being friends.

"Who's that? Why you looking like that?" Jami asked, watching the frown on my face as I looked at my phone.

"Ru," I replied then answered. "Yes?"

"What's up, Amor? You stepping out?"

"Yeah, I'mma hit this Super Bowl game with Jami."

"Oh, okay. I was gon' see if you wanted to roll with me to the homie's shit."

I rolled my eyes because this nigga was full of shit. "Nah, I'm good. I already made plans with my friends."

"A'ight," he replied, sounding sad.

I didn't know what he expected from me because he was still an asshole toward me even after the other day when I finally gave in and gave him some pussy. After putting this good shit on him, I expected him to loosen up, but hell nah. Nigga got right up with that same damn frown. I would say I understood why, but me always running the streets wasn't no damn excuse.

"Let's roll, friend." I looked at Jami because Misha was texting, saying she was in the front. I grabbed my handbag, and we headed out the door.

When we walked out, Mish was out the car rocking her Pittsburgh Steelers dress and thigh-high boots. I checked out her body, and it was banging. For the last few weeks, she had gone to *Revamp Body Studio* for body sculpting. The owner @Bstaypoppin was our dawg from back in the day, so she told us to come through, and she'd hook us up. Misha held up a bottle of Henn and a bottle of Bleu Belaire. I also had three bottles of Hennessy because we definitely didn't walk into any party empty-handed nor leached off muthafuckas. The party was in a warehouse marijuana dispensary, so they weren't tripping off us bringing our own liquor. Which was good because I didn't trust bars. These days, you couldn't tell me they weren't pouring cheap shit into Hennessy bottles.

"Who driving?" I held up the keys to my Porsche truck because I wasn't driving.

I was gonna get fucked up tonight and show my ass. I felt single, and it felt great. I barely talked to Chaotic because I was still in my feelings about the baby he was having, and I definitely wasn't fucking with my baby daddy.

Since Don B and I had been texting, he was pretty much getting my attention. Chaotic was still on my mind heavy, but I coached myself to just let things go. He hadn't been able to catch me at work because it had slowed down, so I wasn't going much. In a couple weeks, it was gonna pick back up due to the IRS opening, so I was sure he would come around. However, I was hoping he'd get the picture and just leave me alone; or, at least that was what I pretended because Lord knows my mind, body, and soul craved attention from him.

"Ohhh, turn that up!" Jami shouted from the back seat.

"This my shit," I replied and turned it up.

We all began singing to Rihanna's "Needed Me."

*"I was good on my own, that's the way it was, that's the way it was
You was good on the low for a faded fuck, on some faded love. Shit,*

what the fuck you complaining for? Feeling jaded huh? Used to trip off that shit I was kickin' to you.
Had some fun on the run though I give it to you..."

We all continued to sing to the next couple of slow songs. Before we pulled into the lot, we changed the music to some trap shit, and it changed our mood.

When we walked into the party, the clouds of smoke met us at the entrance. Before reaching out to Don B, we headed to the bar to get some cups and ice, then found us a table not too far from the television. As soon as we took our seats, all eyes were on us, and the envious stares came from the women. One thing we didn't do was sweat bitches because fighting wasn't something we were doing tonight. I had my 9mm secured in my Raiders purse, and on my daughter, I would air this bitch out. Nine times out of ten, Misha had her gun too, and if I bussed, she would follow suit.

"Hey, Don B!" Jami cooed as Don approached our table.

When I looked up, he had spoken to her, and Mish and was now in my space. I eyed him up and down dressed in a pair of black slim fit Levi's and a 49ers jersey. His locs were freshly twisted, and he had a sleek line up.

"Hey." I smiled shyly and tried to look the other way.

"Don't, 'hey' me. Give me a hug, nigga." He pulled my hands to help me up. He took me into his arms, and, damn, he smelled good. "'Sup wit' you?"

"Nothing. You want a drink?" I offered, hoping he drank dark liquor.

"I'm drinking Remy, but I'll have a drink wit' you."

I began pouring him a cup, and he took a seat next to me. As the girls tuned into the game, Don B and I began to chat. From time to time, I checked my phone because Chaotic had been posting back to back Snaps. He appeared to be at some Super Bowl party, and, of course, his bitch was with him. She made it her business to be in nearly every video, and each time, I rolled my eyes.

"Who you got?" Don B asked, bringing my attention back to him.

"Well, since my team ain't playing, I made a few bets on Brady," I replied, referring to the Patriots QB. Everybody knew Brady was the face behind his team, and because I felt like he was the cartel of football, I placed every bet on him.

"That's what's up. I bet on Pats too. They 'bout to smash these foo's." He looked up at the big screen mounted on the wall.

"Don B!"

We both looked around at the voice who called Don's name. A guy wearing a Pats jersey walked over and gave him a pound.

"HD, what's up, my nigga?"

"Shit, I'm good. Tryna be on like you." The guy's eyes scanned our table, then he looked at me. "How you doing?" he spoke, and I nodded my head.

"That's me, nigga." Don B put his arm around me and chuckled.

"Okay, okay." He looked over at the girls in hopes one was available.

I playfully rolled my eyes at Don B because he already was putting tabs on me. Not that I wanted this nigga, but it was cute.

"Aye, Don, send me them tracks tonight." Another guy walked over and spoke to Don.

"I'll forward them now."

"A'ight. Good looking." The guy ran off over to the TV and began watching the game.

The place was pretty packed, and by the way everyone chanted Don B's name, I could tell he was someone in his section.

"What kind of tracks you got?" I leaned in and whispered to Don."

"I got some cool shit. You wanna hear?" he asked, already pulling up his tracks to send to the guy.

He punched in the info, sent the tracks, and began playing a few for me to hear. I couldn't help but bop my head because they were dope.

"Damn, this hot." I looked at him impressed. "You made this?" He nodded his head, and I was really impressed by his talent. "I'll kill this track." I smiled with confidence.

He looked at me to see if I was serious, and I confidently nodded again. I could tell by the look on his face he didn't think I was serious, so I went to my phone and began showing him all the videos I had on YouTube. All the nights we spent at the studio, I never bothered with telling Don B I could rap. The other guys knew because they recognized me from the "Certified" video.

By the time Don was done watching the videos, he had forgotten all about that game and was now more in tune with the fact I knew how to rap. He was smiling from ear to ear, and I knew he was digging my style of rap.

"Man, you be playing. How come you never mentioned this?"

"I don't know." I shrugged and smiled.

"I think you pretty dope, ma. You need to get back into that booth."

"I don't know. I kinda lost my passion for music."

"Hell nah. You too dope to waste your talent. Let's set up something."

"I'm down," I replied, already thinking 'bout how I was gonna body that track.

He continued to smile, and the more I stared at him, I found him more attractive. I was digging his laid back demeanor and the way he catered to not only me but my girls. He made sure we had ice, the music was good, and any nigga who stood in front the TV he'd make sure we could see. He was always like this at the studio, and I noticed he was to himself a lot. His vibe was just like I liked, but no matter what, I couldn't get Canyon off my mind. I had to shake this feeling, and if entertaining Don B would help, then I would move in on him.

CHAPTER TWENTY FIVE

Chaotic

"Told my lil bro, I had to chase M's
.40 on me, all big face bills
In the back of the Mulsanne, letting the space build
If the police flip me with this Glock, I'mma face ten..."
-Tee Grizzley

"**B**ig, you want greens?"
"I want all that shit, Lady."
"Fat ass." My lady loc laughed as she piled all types of shit on my plate.
"Let me get the keys."
Lady and I looked up to Mercedes, who walked in and

asked for the car keys. Lady rolled her eyes, and I knew it was because of how standoffish Cedes was acting. Not to mention, she had to make my plate because my own bitch wouldn't do it. What Lady didn't know was, Cedes was still in her feelings about me making her have an abortion. Since the day I took her, shit been bad at home. We barely talked, wasn't no fucking, and the bitch wouldn't even cook me a decent meal.

I reached in my pocket and handed her the keys without looking at her. I ain't have too much of nothing to say because I ain't want no baby right now, and either she respected it or got the fuck on.

"What's up with her?" Lady asked when Cedes walked out of the kitchen.

"I don't know. Bad energy." I shrugged because one thing I never did was downplay my bitch to anyone.

"Aye, hoe, let me hold a thou." My little bro walked in and punched me in the chest.

"I'm broke, nigga," I replied to his ass because all he did was break me like he was one of my hoes. Nigga was out here hitting shit and had a cold stash, but no matter how much money he got, he stayed in my pockets.

"Nigga, you up. Run it," he added, and I knew he was serious.

I shook my head and reached into my pocket. "Here nigga, with yo' five-dolla ass." I handed him two bands and grabbed my plate from Lady.

"Good looking." He smiled a wide grin and slapped Lady on the ass.

"How that nigga get his plate before me?" he asked, with his hating ass.

Lady began cursing him out, and that was my cue to leave. I headed back into the living room and took my original seat in front the TV. The Patriots were up by two touchdowns, which was already expected. My boys ain't make it to the Super Bowl, but we damn sure made it to the playoffs. I still repped my team in my Dallas jersey and Dallas fitted hat.

"Hey, Chaotic."

I looked up as I bit into my rib, and a chick by the name of Dior was smiling like she did every time in my presence. I knew she liked me, but just like I did all these bitches, I *sister zoned* her ass so she could get any thoughts of me wanting her out her mind. Don't get me wrong, Dior was very much fuckable, but I didn't chase a big butt and smile. Keep shit gee, all these bitches was in love with a nigga, and they all got the zone. I had a bitch, and until I got the bitch I really wanted, this what it was.

As I continued to eat and watch the game, I sipped my drank and ignored every nigga in the room. It was a house full of people, and believe it or not, I knew everyone, but I ain't give three fucks. The yard was full of people as well because when my lady gave an event, she'd pack shit out. She kept a million bitches around her, and the homies fucked with her heavy because she was the hood princess. My whole Chaotic crew was royalty because we got money and put fear in niggas. My little bro was just like me in a sense. Crazy part, y'all thought I was wild? Nah, that nigga a whole terrorist.

"My nigga, Chaotic!" Mayor walked in, and like always, his voice shook the entire room.

I smiled, happy to see my nigga, so I wiped the BBQ sauce from my hands and stood to my feet. "Mayor, what's up, nigga?"

"Money, nigga. I know you bet on Brady."

"Hell nah, fuck Brady." I laughed because I wasn't a bandwagon type nigga. Brady was praised in the NFL, so I prayed for the Patriots' downfall.

"Ahh, nigga, its only second quarter." He reached in his pocket and dropped a few hunnit on the table.

I did the same and sat back down. Rather Brady lost or not, I wasn't betting on that nigga.

"Nigga, so you got the boy?" Mayor asked in a whisper, speaking on Raphael.

"Hit that nigga where—" I went to say, but the sound of arguing from outside stopped me in my tracks.

Mercedes' voice could be heard, and it sounded too aggressive for my liking. I walked over to the window to see what was going on, and I could see her and one of my homegirls going back and forth. When I noticed the rest of my homegirls standing not too far away, I ran outside.

"What's up?" I walked up on the homegirl who was in her face.

"Yo' bitch! She got a foul ass mouth! You need to check that bitch!"

"I don't need to check shit. You betta pipe down before I make her beat yo' ass." I fumed ready to slap the bitch myself.

I was in her face, and just as I thought, one of her boy cousins ran over to us like he was tough. I stepped right into his face, and before I knew it, the homegirl took off on Cedes, and they began fighting. I ran over to they fight and snatched the bitch back roughly. I didn't give a fuck. My bitch wasn't 'bout to be fighting nor approached by no bitch. I snatched Cedes back and whipped out my strap.

Pop! Pop! Pop! Pop! Pop! Pop! Pop! Pop! Pop!
Pop! Pop! Pop! Pop! Pop! Pop! Pop!

I emptied my whole clip in the air and everyone began scattering.

"Party the fuck over! I advise y'all to get the fuck on because the next shots gon' be in somebody body next round." I pulled my extra clip from my back pocket and slammed it into my strap.

When I looked up, Lady Chaotic was on the porch with her pistol in hand, daring anybody to jump stupid. I swear I loved the fuck out that girl. This was her crib, and she ain't give a fuck about shit but me.

"It's good, Lady. I'm gone," I told her and escorted Cedes out the yard.

We hopped into my whip before the Ones came and pulled

off to head home. The entire way, my blood was boiling. I was gonna drop Cedes off and come right back. I didn't give a fuck about how nobody felt. They knew me, and they knew I didn't play when it came to my bitch. Rather it was Cedes or any bitch, if you were mine, then I'd go to war behind you. Simple.

When I dropped Cedes off, she asked was I good, but I ignored her. I was mad as fuck because of the situations she put me in. Although I'd go to war behind her, it was the fact that I could be sitting in a jail cell behind a bitch who would prolly be gone by the time I got a booking number. Crazy part was, her bitch ass cousin, Tuck, was right there, and the nigga let it all go down. Therefore, I was on my way back to the hood because that nigga had to answer to me.

Instead of going back to Lady's, I pulled up to the park where I knew everyone would be. I cocked my strap before getting out and grabbed the extra two clips. I jumped out and headed into the park where the crowd was, and the first person I noticed was my lil' brother. I could tell he was going up on niggas, and when everyone noticed me approaching, their eyes grew wide.

I walked right over to Tuck and pulled my strap out. I cracked him over the head and began pistol whipping him until he was unconscious. By the time I let up, my chest heaved up and down, and it was like I turned into the Hulk. I looked around the crowd and dared any nigga to say a word. However, amongst the crowd were the niggas I fucked with heavy, so they were rolling with me. I did notice one nigga's, Lil' Beedy, face frowned like he wasn't feeling what just happened.

Before I could run up on him and crack his ass, my little brother already hit him with a powerful blow that sent him crashing into the park table. I stood back and watched my brother demolish the nigga because one thing I didn't do was treat my homies like an enemy. Lil' Chaotic had it under control, so I let him do him. Tuck was leaking on the side line, and Lil' Beedy ain't want no more. Them niggas knew what it was, so when they came to, they lingered around.

I didn't even smoke weed, but right now, I wanted to get high. I took the blunt from Lil' Luke and pulled on it long and hard. Within minutes, shit was back to normal. Well, until I pulled out my phone and went on Snap. I went straight to Amor's post and got mad all over again. She was at a Super Bowl party, and after investigating, I could see her sitting cozy with a nigga. The second video, I recognized the nigga as the same nigga from her job the last time I popped up. *A client, my ass*, I thought because she was a fucking lie. I shook my head, and as bad as I wanted to hit her ass up, I let her be.

I noticed since the day on the beach, she'd been acting weird. I was sure it was because of Cedes being pregnant, but what she didn't know was, that baby was dead and gone. Instead of telling her that, I kept the shit to myself because if she wanted to act weird, then fuck her. I ain't owe nobody an explanation; therefore, I wasn't explaining shit. I knew eventually I would hit her up, but as of right now, fuck her. She could keep entertaining these niggas because soon, I was gon' snatch her dumb ass up with a gun and duct tape if I had to.

CHAPTER TWENTY SIX

Chaotic

"Old niggas on that old shit, it's a young nigga time
A bigger picture, bigger difference, it's a young nigga rhyme
Head over water, he say all he do is step with that iron
Catch that nigga slipping, knock his heart from out his chest with
that iron..."
-NBA Young Boy

R iding down Central Avenue, I looked over to the passenger seat from time to time at Lil' Canyon. He was bopping his head to NBA Young Boy's "Big Talk," and I could tell this was his shit. I watched my son closely because I was still fucked up by how much he had grown.

He was fourteen years old, but his laid back attitude made him appear much older. His mother, along with my mother, did a great job raising him because although he was a thug, he wasn't affiliated with a gang, and he didn't run the streets like most teens. The little nigga did smoke weed, but I was cool with that. If it was one thing I ain't want, it was for him to get sucked in by these wicked streets. He was doing good in school, and all he wanted was his Backwoods and to be fly for the girls.

"Nigga, you weak. I'll smash you in *Madden*," Lil Canyon said into the phone. He was live on Instagram with 300 viewers. "I'm wit' my dad," he added and turned the camera around to show the Maserati emblem on the steering wheel. When he flipped the camera back around, I started clowning him like I always did.

"Nigga, you ain't got no bitches."

"Dad, I got girls." He chuckled and looked back into the camera. "On me, he the one ain't got no girls," he spoke to one of his friends on live, laughing.

"Y'all got me fucked up. I got a bitch." I chuckled, but they really had me fucked up. I pulled out my phone and went to Instagram. I held the phone in his face, so he could see her..

"Bro, that's Amor." He read the name and smiled. "She fire. That ain't you." He chuckled again tryna downplay me to his friends the way I had done him. "Her 'Gram popping. Nigga, that's really not you." He continued cheesing as he clicked on different pictures. []

"What?" I went to Amor's number and pressed send on a FaceTime call.

After about three rings she answered. I observed her background and noticed plenty of green grass. I then took notice of the many tombstones, and that was when I knew she was at the cemetery.

"Hey." She smiled into the camera faintly.

Lil' Canyon was on the side of me smiling because I had proved my point. I focused back on Amor, and I saw a bit of ache

168

in her eyes. I was glad we were pulling up to mom's crib because this gave me a chance to hop out and inquire about why she looked so gloomy. I ain't never saw her like this, so it was doing something to me. No matter how much I noticed I was breaking baby girl down, she always held a poker face. Her energy was always so dope, so seeing her like this was fucking with me. The good thing was, I knew it was because she was at the cemetery and nobody was fucking with her. The way I did niggas the other day for Mercedes, imagine how I'd do for Amor. I'd kill anything that ever tainted her or caused her any harm.

"What's up, ma? You good?" I asked as soon as I closed my driver door.

"Yeah, I'm okay, Canyon," she replied, but I knew that was bullshit because she called me by my government name.

"Why you at the cemetery?"

"I came to see my little brother. It's his birthday," she said and turned the camera around so I could see the headstone. It read *Karter Barkley* with his birthdate and date of death.

"Damn. Sorry for your loss." I was sincere, especially seeing he died at such a young age.

"Thank you."

"No thanks, ma. Hit me when you leave," I told her because I couldn't stand to see her in such a state. I wanted to tell her so bad it was my b-day as well, but I didn't wanna intervene on her time with her brother.

"Okay."

I disconnected the line and ran up the flight of steps to my mother's crib.

"Happy birthday, son!" she yelled when I walked through the door.

"Good looking, ma." I hugged her and noticed a cake and balloons on the table. "Aww, this fa' me?" I smiled because no matter what, my old lady never missed a beat. Even when I was locked up, I got b-day cards, Christmas cards, and Thanksgiving cards.

"Yeah, that's for you. So what you doing tonight?"

"Cedes throwing me a function."

"Ump," she replied because she couldn't stand Cedes. "Yeah, I heard about yo' ass shooting up the Super Bowl."

"They was tripping, ma."

"They always tripping. Just hope them snitching ass niggas don't tell on yo' ass." She held her hand on her hip.

"I'm straight. Trust me."

I walked into the kitchen and washed my hands, so I could eat. Lil' Canyon came back into the room and took a seat with me at the table. We started clowning around with my moms until Lil' Chaotic came, so we could hit the mall and go to the club.

Chaotic's B-day party

"More money, more problems
More guns, more violence
I beat a couple cases, I feel like John Gotti..."

Tossing 500 ones in the air, at a time, toward the strippers, I bobbed my head to Future and took gulps from the bottle of Ace in my hand. A nigga was good and buzzed, and so far, my birthday was still smooth. The night was still young, and to my surprise, Cedes was smiling and enjoying herself. I watched as she tipped the strippers and even popped a few on the ass. Tonight, she had brought her three sisters, so they were turnt up with her.

I had to give it to her. She had my day done up nice, and I didn't expect it. I knew I was having a party, but I didn't expect her to go all out on the decor, strippers, and liquor. She was sitting pretty in a sexy ass dress I planned to tear off her when we got home. She had copped my birthday outfit, so I was looking fresh to death in a pair of red Balenciaga sneaks with the shirt to match. I complimented them with a pair of stone-washed white jeans and a fresh white Henig fur coat that I had taken off.

About thirty minutes later, I noticed a crowd of bottle girls coming in our direction. They carried more bottles and sparkles that lit up the entire club. Another chick rolled a cake in, and when I noticed the ski mask, I smiled. Shit was fly.

"Happy birthday, baby." Cedes walked over and kissed me.

The DJ switched the music to 50 Cents "In Da Club," so my niggas came over to me and began rapping. I sat back with a huge grin because this was the first birthday celebration I'd had in years. I looked around at all my niggas and my girl, and it was the perfect scenery. Everyone I loved was here until I realized I was missing one thing. *Amor.*

Just that fast, my energy changed, but I ain't show it. I waited for everyone to finish singing happy birthday, then excused myself like I had to use the restroom. When I made it to the hall, I pulled out my phone and looked at the time. It was a little before twelve, so I knew there were chances she was home with her nigga. Then again, she was probably out because that was all she'd been doing lately.

"Happy birthday," was the first thing she said when she answered.

"Good looking, baby girl." I smiled. "Where you at?"

"I'm around, Canyon," she replied like she ain't wanna be bothered.

"Amor, quit playing. Where you at?" I tried hard not to turn up on her ass.

"I'm in the hood."

"I need to see you."

"I can't."

"The fuck you mean, 'you can't'?"

"I'm good, Chaotic. Enjoy your birthday, please." She hung up on me.

I looked at my phone and wanted so bad to hit her back, but I didn't. I headed back to the VIP and took a seat. I sat here for a moment, in a daze, and when I finally looked up, Mercedes was watching me. She slightly shook her head as if she could tell my mood changed and why. I just looked at her, and what could I say? Shit. My whole mood did change. I looked at Cedes again and I asked her the question I had been dying to ask.

"What's my favorite soda?" I whispered into her ear over the music.

"Yo favorite soda? Why you ask that?"

"Just answer the question ma."

"Orange, shit I don't know." she shrugged and focused her attention back into the crowd. I shook my head and this help make up my mind.

For the last couple of hours, I sat back and continued to drink. Once the club was nearly closing, I gave my lil' bro and homies a pound, then told Cedes let's roll. When we made it to the whip, I opened her door, and she fell into the seat sadly. I wasn't sure, but I felt the energy from her and knew she felt the way I did; this relationship was pretty much over. The entire ride home, the car was quiet except for the radio that played lowly.

When we pulled up to the crib, Cedes climbed out, then turned to see if I was getting out. My mind told me to just go in the house, but my heart was pulling me in another direction.

"I'll be back," I told her and pulled away from the curb before she could object.

I was going to see my bitch because her snap told me exactly where she was at. Her hood. I didn't give a fuck about her homies because all I wanted was my bitch. At the end of the day, my pops gave his life for them niggas, so them niggas had to give me their princess. It was just that simple.

CHAPTER TWENTY SEVEN

Amor

"He could tell I was wifey material
He was liking my style in my videos
I wasn't lookin' for love, I was lookin' for a buzz
So at times I would lie and say, 'I'm busy,' yo
'Cause it's too much, and it's too clutch
Who wants rumors of the two of us?
But when you're away, I can't get you out of my mind..."

I looked at my ringing phone, surprised that Chaotic was calling. I was so in tune with the lyrics of the song to his new ringtone I nearly didn't answer. This song reminded me of him so much. One night, my phone rang with the ringtone, and Ru looked at me like I was crazy. Because I really didn't give a fuck how he felt, or even if he asked who it was, I left the room to answer. I knew he looked at me weird because of the song ,but he didn't sweat me.

"Happy birthday." I faintly smiled with a slight bit of jealousy.

I'd finally watched his Snaps, and he was out at the club turnt up. His girlfriend stood beside him as a girl rolled out a huge cake. The cake was made with a ski mask, one hundred dollar bills, and a pistol on top. The cake was followed by bottle girls with liquor and sparkles, and they were doing it up. It was crazy because out of all the days of the year, Chaotic shared the same birthday with Karter. I was still in feelings about Karter's death, and this was something I went through every year on his birthday and death date.

"Amor! You guys don't go too far up the street where no one can see you."
"Okay, Mama."
"Come on, Amor, faster, damn. You pushing too slow!"
"Mama said we can't go far."
"We not. We just going to the corner and turn around."
"Okay."

Karter threw his arms in the air and began to scream louder. I pushed him so fast in the metal shopping cart that my mother had stolen from Food 4 Less; my adrenaline was pumping along with his. This was something we did every day because we were too damn big to play with toys

"Good looking, baby girl." I heard Chaotic's voice, and it brought me from my thoughts. "Where you at?"

"I'm around, Canyon," I replied, looking into the sky.

With all the smog in Los Angeles, the air was foggy, but the stars peeked through the fog. The air was breezy, and my mood matched the weather. I was still in my feelings about my lil' brother, so I wasn't in my right mind.

"Amor, quit playing. Where you at?" He spoke lowly, and I could hear it in his voice he was saucy.

"I'm in the hood," I lied.

"I need to see you."

"I can't." I dropped my head and tried to block out the sound of his voice.

"The fuck you mean, 'you can't'?"

"I'm good, Chaotic. Enjoy your birthday, please."

I hung up on him wrapped up in my feelings. I wanted so bad to see him, but I just couldn't. I needed to get that man out my system because he was fucking with my mental.

"Who was that? Yo' little nigga?" I looked over and totally forgot about Don B.

"Yeah," I replied and focused my attention back on the sky. I could hear the snarl he let out because he was in his feelings.

"You in love with that nigga, huh?" he asked and waited for my reply.

"Honestly, yes. It's a very complicated situation."

"Like?"

"Like, I'm more in love with him than the nigga at home. If I could, I'd be with him."

"So what's stopping you?"

Again, I could see the jealousy in his eyes. Don B wanted me in the worst way, but it was like my heart was on reserve. I didn't want no nigga but Chaotic, and if I couldn't have him, I'd stay and deal with Ru's bullshit. Don B was just something to do for the meantime. Don't get me wrong, he was cool as hell; however, the heart wanted what the heart wanted. We were kicking it tough for the last couple weeks, and he was everything I'd want in a man.

"Let's get back inside." Don B opened his door and grabbed the black plastic bag that contained the liquor, ice, and blunts.

We had been in the studio for hours and left to make a store run. This was my third time here, and just like I said, I murdered every track Don B had given me. Our time alone in the studio was what made us bond, but each day, I thought of Chaotic. Don B and I hadn't been intimate, but we did kiss a couple times. As bad as I wanted to fuck him, I held my composure because, like I said, I was saving myself.

"Let's add a double to the second verse."

"Okay," I replied and stepped into the booth.

He turned on the track, and when the second verse came on, I began rapping over the first track I had already done. Don B had begun pouring us a drink, and the minute I was done, I walked out the booth and began sipping my cup. A drank was much needed right now because I needed to unwind and get *him* off my mind. I could tell Don B's energy had changed, so after work was done, I was gonna have him take me to my car.

❤️□□□

"What's up with you?" I asked Don B because he hadn't said much of nothing the entire way to the hood.

I knew what was up with him, but I didn't understand why was he tripping. He wasn't my nigga, and just because our little love affair began to spice up didn't mean I was supposed to stop loving Chaotic. He knew my feelings weren't at home with Ru, so Chaotic was his biggest threat.

"Shit. I'm straight."

"No you ain't, and it shows in your facial expression. Not to mention, you ain't said shit to me in a few hours. Normally, you'd be kissing all over me, and you ain't did all that."

"Shit, it's pointless, keep it real."

"Wow." I laughed, wondering if he was serious. I peeped his facial expression, and the nigga was. "What you want from me?" I asked, and he didn't reply for a brief moment.

"I want you. Leave the nigga at home, and be with me."

Again, I looked to see if he was serious, and he was. The shit sounded stupid as fuck if you asked me because he made it seem like life was just that easy.

"Why me?" was the only thing I could come back with.

"Shit, you cool. I like the way we vibe, and I could see me fucking with you the long way."

"I understand that ,but it's not that easy. And anyway, what you gon' do about yo' bitch?" I asked because the nigga had a whole girlfriend out of state.

From what he told me, they had been together for a few years, and every chance he got, he went to visit. It was kinda like one of those double life things. Nigga had her stashed away in a house out of town, and I guess he thought I was okay with being his Cali bitch. I knew those assumptions also came from the fact that I had Ru, and Chaotic had a girl. He figured I was Chaotic's side bitch, and on the outside looking in, it prolly looked that way. However, what he didn't know was, Chaotic and I had never even been intimate. Our relationship consisted of lust and a bond that was built over time.

"I'mma shake her," he finally replied just as he was pulling up behind my car.

I grabbed my purse and looked at him. "We gon' talk, alright?" I bit into my bottom lip and looked at him. He nodded his head, so I took that as my cue to get out of his car. "I'mma hit you."

I closed the door and headed into the yard. I saw a few homies hanging out, so I decided to stay behind and avoid going home to Ru.

The moment Don B pulled from the curb, my phone rang, and it was Chaotic. I looked at the time, and it was now 2:36 in the morning, which told me he was done partying. Instead of answering, I let the call go to voicemail, and I began making small talk with the homies.

I noticed Boss' hating ass in the cut, and he didn't say two words to me. Once upon a time, Boss and I were thick as thieves. These days, I knew why he acted weird, and it had to do with the rumors that surfaced about Chaotic and I. I knew he'd heard, just like everyone else had heard, that I was creeping round town with dude. It seemed like everyone knew this but Ru, and I knew it was only a matter of time before someone would give him the full details. Ru asked a few times about my social media corresponding with Chaotic, but because we now talked on Snap, it ceased his curiosity.

"Hi, Amor."

I heard a chick's voice, so I looked into the car to see who it was. There were three chicks in total, and I only knew one, which was the girl had spoken my name.

"What's up?" I replied because she said my name as if she knew me like that.

She had only seen me when she pulled up to the hood, and not once had I ever said two words to her.

Me: *Way? I'm on the block?*
Rawdy: *I came to grab my coat. Them bitches still there?*
Me: *Yeah, they here.*
Rawdy: *A'ight, I'm omw.*
Me: *K.*

I put my phone back into my purse and waited for Rawdy to come.

A hot ten minutes passed when she walked up, and by the way the girl in the passenger side looked, I could tell she was the one crushing on Rawdy. These days, it seemed like most women were gay, and these days, they loved masculine woman. Every girl who came to the hood, who was into girls, fell for Rawdy. Not only was she a nice-looking stud, but she dressed well, and her body was flooded in tattoos. Her long hair and light tone made her look like Young MA, and her tough demeanor made her more appealing.

"Why you out this late?" Rawdy asked, walking into the gate.

"Just left the studio."

"That's what I like to hear. I keep telling you stop letting that talent go to waste," she added, sounding like Don B.

"I'm not really on to much with the music shit. I really been doing it for fun lately. I've been coming across some dope tracks, and for *free*." I added emphasis on free.

"Aye, who dis?" the lil' homie, Maniac, asked, looking toward the street. His voice alerted me, and he reached for his pistol.

When I finally looked in the direction of the car, I knew it was Chaotic by the way his fitted cap set on top of his head. I watched the car with ease, not knowing if I should walk out to the front yard. My phone began ringing, and I knew it was him by his ringtone. Before I could answer and tell him it wasn't cool, Boss grabbed his gun and began running towards the front. □

"Chill, Boss!" I yelled out and ran behind him.

By this time, Chaotic had already bussed a U-turn and was in front of the gate.

"I'm 'bout to air this nigga shit out," Boss said, taking aim.

I quickly stepped off the curb and ran to the passenger side of his whip.

"Just go!" I began shouting as he looked at me.

"Man, get the fuck in the car." He spoke in a calm voice. When he noticed Boss had his gun on him, he looked from me to Boss and chuckled. I swear this nigga was bat-shit fucking crazy.

"Boss, put the gun down!" I continued screaming, but Boss wouldn't let up.

"That nigga ain't stupid, cuz," Chaotic said, only making the situation worse.

"Chaotic, go! Just go, nigga!"

This time, I screamed in fear. I knew there were chances Boss would shoot, and out of fear of what Chaotic would do, I just wanted him to pull off.

"Shoot, nigga!" Chaotic sat right here and began taunting him.

I was growing very frustrated, but no matter what, I wasn't moving from in front of the car. By this time, all the homies had come out of the yard. I was hoping these niggas ain't pull out there guns because I wasn't gonna sit here and let them take not a pop shot.

"Exactly what I thought," Chaotic spoke, then looked at me. He lifted up a Ruger 57 to let me know he had his heavy artillery, and I knew this only made Boss angrier. "Take yo' ass home now. On my daddy, you got ten minutes," Chaotic demanded, then pulled off doing about 200.

I let out a deep sigh and turned around to face the backlash.

"You fucking on that nigga and got him thinking he could pull up to the hood. Next time, I'mma kill that bitch ass nigga." Boss fumed.

I had to close my eyes and *woosah* because if it was one thing I hated, it was when anybody referred to Chaotic as a bitch.

"First off, we all know the nigga ain't no bitch. Second, I ain't fucked him, and if I did, my pussy ain't yo' fucking business. All you gon' do is run and tell Ru, and I don't give a fuck. That nigga got just as many rights to pull up over here. His pops died for the hood, nigga!" I screamed to the top of my lungs because this nigga had finally pushed my buttons. He looked at me, but he didn't say a word, so I continued. "That same muthafucking nigga name tatted on your arm is his damn father. So respect it. I don't give a fuck about what y'all do and the bitches y'all bring around. You think I don't know them hoes from across the tracks!" I made sure to say it loud enough for the bitches in the car to hear. Frustrated, I pulled out my strap and held it to my side. "Now, I'll be wrong if I air these bitches shit out, right?"

Boss looked at me because he knew I wasn't playing. He also knew if I pulled my pistol, out nine times out of ten, I'd use it. However, I was just showing him the bullshit he was pulling could go both ways.

"Chill, Amor," Rawdy finally spoke up because she knew what would be the outcome.

The bitches in the car watched me with fear, but I wasn't even on that. The homies stayed fucking with our enemies, and out of all the homegirls, I was one who minded my damn business. Not to mention, they kept Ru in one of their many fuck sessions, and not once did I ever attack them. I went after Ru because Ru was the nigga I was fucking.

Everyone stood around with nothing to say. Once the crowd went silent, I walked off for my car, and Boss finally spoke up. Nigga made sure to say that shit so I couldn't hear, and that was the only reason I kept walking. I was done with this shit, and I was definitely done with Chaotic's crazy ass. This nigga was just with his baby mama, yet look at the bullshit he was putting me in. I was done all the way around, so I took my ass home knowing I was gonna have to face Ru. Boss' bitch ass would definitely call and tell him, and just like I defended Chaotic to Boss, I would do the same with Ru.

CHAPTER TWENTY EIGHT

Amor

"Soon as you out a niggas' lives is when they start to miss you
They see you doin' good, now it's kinda hard to diss you
Niggas be sick when they remember all the bad they wished you
Niggas be mad when they can't come and live lavish with you..."
-Nicki Minaj

Valentine's Day

"**W**ho the fuck is DB!"
I opened my eyes to the sound of Ru's voice. At first, I couldn't make out what was

going on until I realized he was holding my phone. I looked at him like he was crazy and jumped up from the bed.

"Give me my shit!" I snatched my phone from his hand.

I looked at the messages that were open, and the nigga had went down the entire thread. Because he didn't ask about Chaotic, I knew he didn't see those messages; dumb nigga there. Had he opened the messages between Chaotic and I, I would have woken up with a pistol in my mouth. There wasn't a day that went by where we didn't say *I love you*. Another thing about Chaotic was, even with his asshole attitude, he still opened up to me about how he felt. We basically poured our hearts out to each other, and no matter how much time we took apart, the love never diminished. I hadn't spoken to him since the day he pulled up in the hood, but he made sure to watch every Snap I posted.

"So you fucking this nigga!" Ru shouted, bringing me from my thoughts.

"No." I climbed back into bed, knowing I had to get ready for work.

"You a muthafucking lie. Y'all hook up almost every fucking night. Yeah, that's where the fuck yo' ass been!"

"Damn, you act like you give a fuck," I threw over my shoulder. "And I been in the studio. That's where I been," I added, sounded like a whole nigga.

"Studio, my ass," he mumbled and stormed out the room.

I lay back on the bed, and I began to feel bad. I wanted so bad to say fuck Ru, but that little bit of love I still had left made me feel bad. I knew after seeing those messages, he was definitely gonna leave my ass. Keep shit real, I was surprised he hadn't been left. I spent every day not only running the streets, but in the studio, for days at a time. I'd come home at two, even three in the afternoon the next day. Over the course of a few weeks, I had been kicking it tough with Don B, and, of course, it was to keep my mind off Chaotic. Therefore, those messages weren't just about working in a studio. We would text each other when we weren't together with *I miss you* and even *thinking about you* messages.

I lay still, lost in my thoughts for quite some time, and I hadn't heard a peep from Ru. I finally got the willpower to get out of bed because I only had an hour to get ready for work. I quickly jumped into the shower and moved around my room trying not to wake Heaven. She was sound asleep in my bed and had just gone to sleep at nearly four this morning.

When I got done dressing, I grabbed my belongings and headed for the door. Ru was sitting on the sofa, and because of my guilt, I couldn't even look at him. I walked out and hopped into my car, and before pulling off, I turned on my YouTube playlist.

"Look, now, if I was yours, and you was mine
Would you do me like you do him and have someone on the side?
So, keep yo' nigga, while I stay on my grind
Just hit me up and we gon' spend some time…"

I couldn't help but listen to the lyrics and smile to Nipsey Hussle's "If You Were Mine." It was a trip that this was the first song that came on, and Chaotic had always played it when we were together. I didn't know why, but this song had always done something to me. I could tell he was rapping to me, and it always sent an exhilarating feeling through my body.

I played the song two more times, then moved on from it because I was getting tempted to call him. It took everything in me not to reach out, and believe me when I say it was hard. Because I didn't want him to know I was watching him, I made a fake Snap and watched him from there. He was always at home with his bitch, but I did notice he was always in the living room alone. He barely posted her, and when he did, I'd look hard to see if her belly was growing. She always wore big clothing, so it was hard to tell, and anyway, she was only about a couple months.

When I pulled up to the job, there were a few people already at the door waiting. We didn't open until ten, and it was 9:50. Instead of keeping them waiting, I took them inside and had them fill out the data entry sheet. When I took a seat at my desk, there was a small teddy and balloon on each desk, and this told me they had come from the boss. Looking at all the teddys made me remember it was actually Valentine's Day, and it tripped me out. Normally, I would go all out for V-day with Ru. We've done everything from helicopter rides to yachts. V-day was probably the only day out of the year Ru and I showed any intimacy.

Welp, there goes my V-day, I thought because I knew Ru wasn't fucking with me. I pulled out my phone and at least sent him a happy V-day text. When I realized he wasn't gonna reply, I called my first client and began working. Shortly after, Jami had come in, and a new girl by the name of Hena. I was happy because it would make the work day easier. Hena really didn't know how to do taxes, but she helped out inputting all the data and anything else Jami and I needed.

Just like I said, the day had gone by smoothly, and by the middle of the day, I was feeling the love of Valentine's Day. Well, a little because the one person who could have fulfilled my day was Chaotic, and he hadn't. Don B had flowers delivered, along with an oversized teddy I could barely carry. I smiled when I saw the gifts, but they wouldn't fill the joy if they didn't came from Canyon. I pulled out my phone to send Don B a text and thank him.

Me: Thanks for the flowers and teddy.
DB: You welcome.
Me: Where did you go? Why you leave?
DB: I had some shit to handle.
Me: Oh, okay.
DB: I'll try to get up with you later.
Me: Okay.

Just as I set my phone back down, I looked up, and Ru was walking through the door. To my surprise, he was holding a V-day basket with a teddy and other things I couldn't see. A slight smile eased up my face until I noticed the change in his facial expression. He looked down at the large teddy bear, then all the things on my desk from my coworkers and frowned.

"My coworkers. I won this here in a contest," I lied. I was already in enough shit, so I wasn't gon' be tough.

"Happy Valentine's Day." He set the basket down, so I stood to my feet. I walked around my desk and placed a kiss on his cheek that took him by surprise. "I'm finna go get the baby. What's up? You gon' let us take you out?"

"Yeah, I guess," I replied, knowing his little game. If he used my baby, then I would go, and he knew that.

"A'ight. I'mma run and get her. Tell yo' boss you leaving for the day."

"Okay."

I started cleaning up my work station. A part of me really ain't wanna go because I didn't wanna act fake in love because it was the holiday. The day consisted of love, and love between Ru and I had died right along with chivalry and fidelity.

Chaotic

"**A**ye! Yo' phone keeps ringing."

I woke up out of my sleep, and Cedes had my phone.

"I'll call her later." I ignored my mom's call and rolled back over sleepy as fuck. I knew I wasn't going back to sleep, so I lay here for a moment until I got up.

Last night, for the first time in a while, Cedes and I kicked it in the house. Because it was Valentine's Day, I decided to cater to her. I cooked her steak and seafood, bought her a few gifts, and even flooded our entire bedroom with rose petals. We poured up a few bottles of Ace and pretty much vibed out with oldies. Although the night was smooth, and we were finally getting along without any arguments the entire time I watched her, my mental fucked with me.

It was like I had finally come to terms with myself that we weren't ever gon' be in love. I mean, I been figured it out, but if a day like Valentine's Day couldn't make us show each other love, then it was definitely over. It wasn't just me. It was Cedes too. Her demeanor and standoffish attitude told me she was sick of me. Ever since that damn abortion, shit was only getting worse. We had roses, liquor, and the perfect music playing, and the entire time, I watched Amor's Snaps while Cedes scrolled through her phone. She had even put on some lingerie, but my dick didn't even get hard. I ended up passing out, and I didn't even turn in my sleep through the night.

I lifted up from the bed, and after handling my hygiene, I went straight to the shower. Once I was done, I slid into my clothes and left the house before Cedes got up. After pulling off, I pulled out my phone to call my mom because she had called nine times.

"I been calling you. The police came by here looking for

you." She spoke in a panic.

"What they say?"

"It was the detectives. They left a card and said they wanted to just ask you some questions. Son, you know that's bullshit."

"I already know, ma. A'ight, I'll get the card. I'm on my way there now."

"Okay."

I hung up the phone wondering what the fuck they could have possibly wanted. I knew it ain't have shit to do with none of the robberies because they would have raided her crib instead of showing up talking about questions. The minute I hung up with my mom, Cedes called.

"'Sup?"

"'Sup. Umm, are we still going to Puerto Rico?"

"Yeah, why?"

"Because you need two forms of ID."

"A'ight, well I got my jail ID, and my driver's license."

"Okay."

"Moms just hit me and said the detectives came by looking for me."

"What they want?"

"Shit, I don't know."

"Oh, okay," she replied wit' not an ounce of sympathy or remorse.

I disconnected her and turned my music on, so I could get my thoughts together. Believe it or not, I wasn't even worried about the police. My mind was more on Amor and how shit had been going these last few weeks. Then, last night, I watched her snaps, and she looked like she was on her family shit. She was out wit' her nigga and her baby, so thoughts of that nigga fucking her at the end of the night had me tripping.

I knew she was still caught up over Cedes being pregnant, but it seemed like the shit with her homies a couple weeks ago only added. Amor knew what type of nigga I was, and she knew when it came to her, I ain't give a fuck. Her homie called himself on some fake tough shit and that didn't do shit but make me laugh. I knew Boss, and one thing I knew for sure, that nigga wasn't no killa. Don't get me wrong, he had a little name over there, but he was a hustla. One thing I knew, hustlas were hustlas, and they were scared of the killers and robbers.

I pulled up to Amor's job contemplating if I wanted to go inside. I sat here for a brief moment and decided to just go in. I climbed out my whip and headed inside straight for her desk. She didn't have any clients, so I was able to approach her.

"What's up?" I asked, and she looked up. I eyed all the shit on her desk, and it only made me mad. "Who got you all this? Yo' little niggas?" I asked, and she frowned.

"My boss and co-workers. Why does it matter? You ain't buy me shit? You was busy dropping roses for the next bitch. Oh, my bad, yo' baby mama." She rolled her eyes, and I chuckled.

"You just like hearing yo' self talk, huh? First, that ain't my baby mama because I been made her get rid of it. Yeah, I dropped roses, but I ain't fuck her. You so worried about that little shit, Amor, fuck them roses because when the time comes, I'mma give you the world."

I walked out just like I always did leaving her ass stuck. I heard her say some smart shit, but I didn't bother turning around. I meant exactly what I said and wasn't shit else to be said. She was tripping off roses, flowers, and shit when I had the world prepared for her. After seeing her with her nigga last night ,I knew it was time I made my move. I could tell it was only a matter of time they would work shit out and possibly work on their family. Therefore, like I said before, I had my duct tape ready, and I was coming out with my gun smoking and my bitch.

CHAPTER TWENTY NINE

Chaotic

"Gotta let you know how I'm feeling
Own my heart, and she just renting
Don't turn away, pay attention
I'm pouring out my heart, girl..."
-Chris Brown

Slam!

I shook my head hearing the door to the bedroom for the tenth time in the last hour. We had just gotten back from our trip, and after I spent nearly fifty-k the bitch should have been in the best spirits. Instead, she walked around with her face balled up and was slamming doors. I swear the energy was bad in this house. So bad I was in the process of plotting my last lick. All I wanted to do was bang something one last time so I could shoot Cedes a couple dollas and leave her.

I could have walked away and just said fuck her, but because I wasn't no fucked up nigga, I decided to just leave her with something before I go. Because of her daughter, and me causing her to lose her job, I was gonna leave her the crib and go cop me something else. 🗆

We were gone on our trip for four days, and the entire trip we barely said four words to each other. I pretty much hung out by the ocean alone, and when it was time for bed, I slept in the second room. I couldn't figure this girl out for the life of me. I wasn't sure if it was because we rushed into a relationship, that we never got a chance to learn one another first. One thing I hated was bad energy, and she had that. Granted, I was in love with someone else, but she ain't know that. I never disrespected her or made her feel like I was gonna shake her. I gave her a chance to love me, and now that I knew that was impossible, it was time I shook.

I lifted up from the sofa and went to look in the fridge. When I realized wasn't shit in there, I opened the freezer and began browsing. I pulled out a pack of steaks and set them in the sink. Because I didn't know how to cook, I was gonna make Cedes get her ass in here. I walked into the room, and because I walked quietly, she never heard me coming. She dropped her phone between the pillows, but it was too late I saw her. Before she could move, I quickly dove over the bed and picked it up.

"Fuck you in here talking to you hiding yo' phone and shit?" I began scrolling through her shit. Of course, I went through her snap first. Because of my guilt, I knew that was where all the dirt went down.

"Give me my fucking phone!" She started screaming and

trying to reach for her phone.

I went to the last snap, and because they disappeared, wasn't shit there. However, I could see the bubbles, so that let me know the nigga was writing something.

Snap

I love you too. I wish you could be with me tonight.

"Oh, you got a nigga you love, but you still in my shit," I looked at her and said with the most calm voice. I dropped her phone on the bed and didn't give her a chance to reply because I really ain't give a fuck.

I walked back into the living room and began searching for my keys. Before I could walk out, Cedes came out of the room and jumped in my face.

"That's my homie," she tried to lie, but that was bullshit.

"Bullshit. He wanna be with you tonight. Tell him you on yo way." I tried to walk past her, but she wouldn't let me.

"Where the fuck you think you going?"

"The fuck away from here. Go be with yo' homie."

"Oh, so you 'bout to run to yo' little blood bitch! Fuck you, Canyon!" She stopped me in my tracks just hearing *blood bitch*.

"Yeah, that's exactly where I'm going." I chuckled and tried to walk out again.

"Run! Run to that ugly ass hoe!"

"Man, you and I both know she ain't ugly. And hoe? Nah, baby girl, that's what she ain't. Trust me, if she was a hoe, I would've been got that pussy." I laughed again and walked past her.

Boom!

My head fell to the side, and it made me spin around. I grabbed the back of my shit trying to process what just happened. I looked at Cedes, and the petrified look on her face verified she had hit me.

"Stupid bitch!" I ran up on her, and without thinking clearly, I slapped her so hard she flew back into the kitchen. I then ran up on her and wrapped my hand around her neck. "If you ever in yo' muthafucking life..."

I was choking her so hard her eyes rolled to the back of her head. I was trying to kill this bitch. I choked her for so long she started turning blue, and the only thing that brought me back to reality was the sound of her daughter crying. I released her neck and stepped back. I shook my head in pure disgust because I couldn't believe we had got to this point. Putting my hands on her was something I never thought I'd do, and now look.

Yeah, it's time to leave, I thought and walked away from her. I went to my bedroom and began tossing some things into a bag. I wasn't gonna take everything now ,but a few pieces of clothing and everything of value was coming with me. I opened my safe and pulled my money out. I left her about twenty grand on the dresser and headed for the door. When I realized my whip was at my mom's crib, I began contemplating my next move. Because of the trip, we were in a rental car, and since it was in her name, I thought against taking it. I pulled out my phone and sent Amor a text. I knew I could have called anyone else in the world, but for some reason, I felt the need to run to Amor. I needed her right now to calm the storm in my ass.

Me: *Aye, ma, come get me.*

Five minutes later.

Gutta Baby: *Come get you? Come get you from where?*
Me: *Home. I need you bad.*
Gutta Baby: *Right now?*
Me: *Yes, now! 3053 S Sawdale Lane 93501.*
Gutta Baby: *It says 49 minutes. I'm on my way.*
Me: *A'ight.*

I stuck my phone in my pocket and went to sit in my garage. I wasn't going back in the crib, so I was gonna sit right here and wait.

CHAPTER THIRTY

Amor

"Gotta let you know how I'm feeling
You own my heart, he just renting
Don't turn away, pay attention
I'm pouring out my heart, oh boy..."
-Nicki Minaj

After going over my last adlibs, I stormed out of the booth and grabbed my purse. I waited for Don B to finish playing the song and give me the confirmation everything was done.

"That shit sounds good."

I looked over to the sofa, and his girlfriend was bobbing

her head to my song. I rolled my eyes without replying and began texting with Chaotic.

"That's a wrap." He spun around in his chair and smiled. He looked me in the eyes, and he knew I was pissed. He wanted to say something so bad, but he couldn't because the bitch was all in our grill.

"I'm out."

I walked out the door, and my mind was made up. I wasn't ever coming back. I knew it seemed like I was on some hater shit, but I wasn't. I wasn't feeling the way Don B was trying to play games like I was a fucking kid. I hadn't seen him since Valentine's Day, and this explained exactly why. His bitch was in town, and all of a sudden, it was all about work. Imagine my surprise when I walked into my studio session, and she was sitting on the sofa. No warning, no nothing. The nigga had the nerve to act excited about seeing me, and that shit irritated me more.

I should have known something was up when I asked him what he was doing on V-day, and he mentioned he had shit to do. After that, no call, no show. He even missed my session days after. Therefore, after today, he didn't have to worry about me again.

I climbed into my car and turned on my music. I then punched in the address that Chaotic had given me and smiled hard inside. I hadn't seen much of him, and the way I was feeling, this was right on time. I needed Chaotic, and I needed him now. It was crazy how no matter what I went through in the world, Chaotic was the only person who could give me that rush I needed. He always took away my problems, and with him, I'd forget about everything in my life. However, what was crazy was, he wanted me to pick him up from his crib. I knew his bitch lived there, so either they broke up, or he just didn't give a fuck. Whatever the case was, it wasn't my concern. I had my strap in my purse for "just in case" purposes.

As I drove to Chaotic's crib, I sipped my brown liquor

from my straw and vibed out to Rihanna's "Wild Thoughts." The GPS said forty-nine minutes, but the way I drove, I was there in thirty. I sent him a text that I was out front, and the garage opened. He walked out of it holding two bags. I popped the truck for him and jumped over to the passenger side so he could drive. I wanted to sip my drank and relax.

"'Sup?" he said when he climbed in. I knew something was wrong because his shirt looked out of place, and a few scratches were visible on his neck.

"You good?" I asked concerned because he appeared to be kinda out of it.

"Yeah, I'm straight." He looked at me and faintly smiled.

I knew better. He wasn't okay, so I was gonna give him some space. He pulled off from his home, and we hopped on the highway and drove until it ended.

The smell of the ocean seeped through the windows, and this told me exactly where we were. The beach. *He definitely has a lot on his mind*, I thought, looking in his direction. That was something else I learned about this man. When he had shit on his mind, he'd drive out to the beach. Right now, this was the perfect place because I wanted to talk to him and see where things were gonna go. I was tired of the back and forth games, and if we were rocking, then we needed to be one. I was tired of stringing Ru along, and it was clear he wasn't in love.

"Here, ma." Chaotic wrapped his coat around my arms.

He closed my door and grabbed me around my waist. He led me out by the water and laid down the small Dallas Cowboys throw blanket he carried. I took a seat, and he joined me. For a moment, we both just looked out into the dark ocean and let the currents of the waves soothe us. When he took my hand into his, it made me smile because it was right on time. I lay my head on his shoulder, and we began talking.

"So what's going on with you and yo' girl?" I asked in

hopes he would finally tell me.

He bit into his lip, then looked out into the water. "It's pretty much over." He shrugged like it wasn't nothing.

"What happened, nigga?"

"Nothing really. Just bad energy. I'm not the type of nigga who walks around mad all the time, ma. I mean, I know I'm an asshole, but I'm a good nigga, and I just wanna be happy. Not only me, but I'mma do everything I can to make my bitch happy as well. Therefore, when I drop roses, I expect the same. It's like I go out of my way to make her happy, and I had to just realize that she ain't happy with me."

I listened as he talked ,and I could relate. I never told him about the problems I was having with Ru, and I felt the same way he did. I bent over backwards to make Ru happy, and nothing worked. It took for me to act like a slut and stay gone until the wee hours for him to get some act right.

"So are you gonna just give it all up?"

"I got too. Amor, I can't keep living a lie with ol' girl. A nigga in love with you, so really, I can't put all the blame on her. My *don't give a fuck* attitude prolly play a part in it too. I believe in my heart that attitude comes from loving yo' ass."

"Well, the feeling's mutual." I looked at him, and he finally turned to meet my eyes. "Believe it or not, Canyon, I'm in love with you too. Things at home fucked up, and no matter how hard I try, they just won't get better. At some point, I gave up."

"Shit, I could tell."

"And how's that?" I smiled because this nigga was too sharp.

"For one, you in the kitchen cooking every night alone. Two, if the home was happy, yo' ass wouldn't be running the streets, all in studios fucking with yo' fake manager. Those signs of unhappiness."

"You right." I looked away from him because a lone tear slid down my cheek. I wasn't in my feelings about Ru; I was in my feelings because of the power of a man. I desired this man something crazy, and it was like my heart surrendered to him. He had supreme power over me, and it was starting to kill me slowly. "So what now?" I asked as a pool of tears began to fall.

I heard a small sigh escape his lips, and he looked out into the ocean. He got lost in his thoughts for a moment, then looked at me. He looked me in my eyes, and I could tell he was searching for a sense of tranquility. I assumed he found it because he pulled my face into his and kissed me. In an instant, my nipples grew hard, and my pussy began to jump. I took it upon myself to lie back, and he took that as his invitation. He climbed on top of me and began tracing my neck with tender kisses. He lifted my shirt and moved down to my stomach. He continued to kiss me, and it was like my body caught fire. My heart began racing because it felt surreal.

"Lift up," he spoke above a whisper, instructing me to lift my bottom, so he could slide my shorts off.

Doing as told, I swallowed the lump in my throat and prepared myself for what was next. Chaotic took off his pants, followed by his briefs, not bothering to care we were out in the open. It was nearly three a.m., so the beach was quiet, but you never knew who was lurking. My eyes fell down to his dick, and my heart began to beat faster. I took it into my hand as if it were a missing piece in the museum. It was long with a curve that I knew would touch a wall that'd never been touched. It was nice and thick, and with the small amount of moonlight shining, I was able to make out the perfection of his throbbing head. It was beautiful.

"You know once I slid in here, it's mine, Amor?" He had this deranged look in his eyes like he would murder the world if I gave my love to anyone.

"Yes," I cried out, anticipating the feeling.

He took the tip into his hand and put it at the opening of my pussy. There was no need to get it wet because I had already caused a wave kinda like the one in front of us.

"Damn, yo' pussy tight." He frowned as he tried to insert himself.

"Ahhhhhhh!" I screamed out, not knowing if I would be

able to handle the rest of him. "Babyyyy...it hurts."

"Relax, baby girl." He slowed down and continued to pry his way in.

"Ohhhhhhh, shit..."

I was finally able to relax, so I parted my legs wider. He began to thrust inside of me, and with every stroke, I died. For the first time in my life, I felt like I was being ripped open. The only thing that helped ease my pain was the fact that I had yearned for this dick for an eternity.

"Yo' pussy soooo wet, ma. Damn, yo' pussy wet."

He continued to stroke. He bit into his bottom lip and caught a rhythm that felt like some porn star shit. This told me he was very much experienced, and I kinda got jealous knowing someone else had gotten this.

"Babyyyyyy...ahhhhh, shit. Baeee." I began fucking him back from the bottom, and I could feel the heat growing, letting me know I was about to cum. "Canyon...I'm...I'm...Ohhh, shit, I'm about to nut, baby!" I began panting and digging my nails into his back.

"Let that shit out, ma." He spoke smoothly and took his thumb to massage my clit. This only added to my orgasm, and a gush of fluid flew out of me.

"Come here." He lifted off me and turned me around. He lay me flat on my stomach and slid back inside of me. Before he began pulverizing me, he used his hand to slightly arch my ass. Instead of going fast, he began hitting me with nice, long strokes while he kissed the back of my neck. "You love me?"

"Yes," I cried out in pure ecstasy.

"Tell me you love me, now," he demanded, but not missing a beat.

"I love you. Oh my God, I love you."

"You promise?"

"I...I...promise, Canyon."

"With no scars?" he asked, and, damn, that shit made my head spin.

"Yes, with no scars," I replied, and it was like this was all he needed to hear.

He began speeding up his pace, and when he found that one perfect rhythm, I knew this was gonna make him nut. I suddenly found my willpower and tooted my ass more to give him extra access to my pussy.

"There she go." He opened my ass wide and found his sacred place. He began going harder and harder, and I could feel his dick growing bigger. The tip was ready to explode. "Grahhhhh-hhhhh!" His voice sounded out and echoed through the night's air.

He continued to go fast trying hard to release every drip of nut inside of my swollen tunnel. When he was done, he softly bit me on my back and rolled over to the side of me. We lay here for a brief moment trying to catch our breath.

"Put yo' clothes on." Again, he demanded in a jealous rage.

I slid my panties on, then my shorts.

"Now lie down." He pulled me under him and threw his arm over me.

"Why you ain't put yo' clothes on?"

"Because I'm a man. I'm straight. If somebody walk up and see yo' pussy, I'mma kill 'em," he spoke, and I could tell the nigga was serious. "I love you, Gutta Baby."

"How much?"

"Too damn much," were his last words, and before I knew it, I dozed off.

When Chaotic and I opened our eyes, the sun was rising giving the sky the most alluring look. I looked at him, and he was already awake. He was lying on his back, and now that I was awake, he turned to his side to look at me.

"Have you been to sleep?"

"Nah."

"Canyon, you need some sleep."

"I'll sleep later, ma. I wasn't 'bout to go to sleep on this beach and something happened to you out here," he replied, brushing a strand of hair from my face. "You ready to go?"

"Yes. I need to shower." I lifted up, and I couldn't help but smile. This crazy ass nigga had a pistol in his hand and one on the side of him.

"A'ight. I'mma take you to my mom's crib. While you in the shower, I'mma run to the mall and grab you a dress or something to throw on."

"Okay," I replied, feeling like I was being kidnapped. I wanted to ask why I couldn't just go home and get dressed, but I knew better than to challenge him.

We lifted up from the blanket and began collecting our things. We then headed to the car and climbed in. I powered on the music while he got the sand out of our shoes. Once done, we got on the highway. As he always did, he took my hand into his and squeezed it tight. I looked out the window still in a zone. It all felt like a magical dream, but the way my pussy was throbbing let me know this shit was real in the flesh.

"I love you, Amor."

"I love you too." I smiled, loving how he always told me he loved me.

"How much?" he asked, making me laugh.

"Too muthafucking much." I replied, and he chuckled. "TMM, nigga," I added, and this was gonna be my new thing.

"I need a gangsta
To love me better
Than all the others do
To always forgive me

Ride or die with me
That's just what gangsters do..."

"You hungry?" He turned the music down briefly.

"Kinda."

"A'ight, we gon' grab something to eat before we go in." He exited the highway and turned right on Central Avenue. "I'mma slide by my G Moms house real quick. Put these straps up."

"Okay," I replied, and he started the song over and turned it up.

I loved this song because it reminded me of our love story. It was Kehlani's "Gangsta" from the *Suicide Squad*. I knew it sounded weird, but Chaotic and I's love story reminded me of The Joker and Harley Quinn's love story. This man would terrorize the world, and the only thing he loved was Harley Quinn. He was afraid to love, and after Harley basically tortured him with her heart, he had no choice but to love her. Harley loved him to the point he made her jump into acid, and she did. Not being able to hide the love he had grown for her, he jumped in to save her.

"Damn," he said, looking in the rearview mirror, bringing me from my thoughts.

"What?" I asked and looked behind us. There was a patrol car behind us, and it had just turned on its sirens.

"Give me the guns," I told him, and he hesitated. "Canyon, now," I demanded, and he slid them over to me without much movement. I put them into my purse and made sure to take my wallet out in case they wanted my license.

"License and registration," the officer asked, walking up to the car.

Chaotic handed it to the officer, and he stepped away from the car briefly. When he came back, he instructed Chaotic to step out the car. He looked at me and began shaking his head. He did as told and stepped out of the car. By the time the officer walked him over to the curb, a swarm of officers rushed into us and jumped out with their guns drawn.

"Passenger, step out of the car with your hands up!" They began shouting into the bullhorn.

I stepped out of the car with my hands in the air and stepped over to the curb. After a few moments, the officers rushed Chaotic and didn't dare cuff me. A female officer wrapped her arm into mine and pulled me to the side.

"Canyon Betterman, you're under arrest for the murder of Karter Barkley." I heard an officer say, and it made me spin around fast.

Karter Barkley. I repeated the words as if I didn't hear him correctly. I looked at Chaotic, and our eyes met. There was so much regret in his eyes that it made me dizzy. We continued to hold each other's gaze, and a pool of tears began to fall from my eyes. I had to be dreaming. No, fuck that. I had to be having a nightmare. My heart began fluttering with pain, and I couldn't help but look Chaotic in the eyes. When the officers snatched him up and walked him to the car, I followed him with my eyes every step of the way.

They stuffed him down into the car, and another officer climbed into the driver seat and wasted no time pulling off. All of the other officers got into their vehicles leaving me standing here. I didn't know what to do next because I was still in shock. They never searched me, and this told me they got exactly what they wanted.

When I finally came to, I climbed into my car and sat here for what felt like forever. The sound of my phone snapped me out of it, and because it was Ru, I let it go to voicemail. I started my engine, and before I could pull off, I began screaming to the top of my lungs...

"Noooooooooooooooo!"

Epilogue

Amor

F or three days, I buried myself inside my bedroom in tears. It was hard because Ru couldn't figure out what was wrong, and I knew I was killing him. Everything that had happened was hard to process, and my heart still ached. A part of me wanted answers, but the other part of me wanted blood. I wanted to kill Chaotic for more than one reason. I asked myself if he knew this entire time and was this all set up to begin with.

I didn't understand why. I mean, I knew I was his enemy, but I ain't deserve no shit like that. I gave that man my heart, and not only that, but my love. The way he told me he loved me was what had me caught up. *He looked so sincere. It couldn't be fake.* I began to cry again and buried my head into my pillow.

When my phone began ringing, I didn't have the strength to answer. I knew it could only be Misha or Jami because I had told them what happened.

(713) 297-6111

I looked at the number that wasn't stored and answered.

"Hello?"

"This is global tel. You have a prepaid call from *Chaotic*. To accept, press five. To deny charges, hang up now, or to block all future calls, dial zero."

Hearing his voice made my blood begin to boil. It took everything in me not to push five and curse him out. However, I couldn't face him. I knew my little brother wasn't the intended victim, but it happened, and I'd never get him back. For years, it fucked with me, and I always promised myself if I found out who pulled the trigger, they were dead. *Fuck Chaotic.*

I got up from my bed and headed into the restroom. When I looked into the mirror, my eyes were puffy from crying, and I looked like a lost soul. I began washing my face and tried hard to get myself together. It was time I faced Ru, but I wasn't gonna tell him the truth.

I took slow steps toward the living room, and with every step, my heart rate sped up. When I turned the corner, my hands began to shake, but a sense of calm came over me when I looked at my daughter. Ru sat on the sofa with Heaven in his arms. I sat back for a moment and just watched them. It was evident in Ru's face that I had broken him down to the point of no return. I knew I'd stressed him out over a course of months, but no matter what, he deserved it. I guess after all this, it made me open my eyes to reality.

Chaotic was really the myth I always pictured him to be. I guess the Harley and Joker story did remind me of us because it was all a tale. My life was right here with Ru, and it was time we had that talk.

I took a seat next to Ru, and neither of us said a word. I turned to face him as I searched for the right words. I let out a soft sigh and turned my whole body around so he could look at me.

"So what you wanna do? You wanna fix this, or just let it go?" I asked seriously. If he chose to let go, then I was fine with that because maybe I needed to be alone.

"Let's fix it," he spoke, and for the first time, I heard sincerity in his voice.

"You wanna move?"

"Yep. Let's go."

"Okay," I replied, and that was all I needed to hear.

I lifted up from the sofa and headed into my bedroom. I sat on the bed and began contemplating my next move. It was time I took my family away from here, and maybe it would help Ru and I's relationship. There was nothing in the city for us, and the way my heart felt, I needed to escape the pain. I needed to find a way to protect my peace, and staying here wasn't gonna work. Therefore, I was gonna start looking for a home a couple hours away. I guess this was what it was gonna be. Who would have ever thought that my fate would end with Ruger?

TO BE CONTINUED...

PART 2 TO LOVING A CHAOTIC SAVAGE

"DEAR CHAOTIC" COMING OCTOBER 21st 2021

Trap Gyrl 1-3

Trap Boy (Trap Gyrl part 4)

Cash Lopez (Trap Gyrl part 5)

A Cold December With Jackie Snow 1-3

Trap Princess (Trap Gyrl part 6)

Me U & Hennessy (Stand-alone)

A Thugs Worth 1-3

BME 1-2 (A Thugs Worth spin off)

The Real Dope Boyz of South Central 1-3

Barbie & Clyde 1-3

Hot Girl Summer In Cali 1-2

Santa Blessed Me With A Bay Area Boss (stand-alone)

Wife of A Compton Savage (stand-alone)

Stealing The Plugs Heart (stand-alone)

A Boss Got Me In My Feelings But A Savage Got My Heart (stand-alone)

Heartbreak In The Hood (Volume 1)

Riding Shotgun With A Boss (Stand-alone)

Justice & Champion (stand-alone)

Treacherous (Stand-alone)

A Billionaire And His Bitch (Stand-alone)

A Billionaire And His Barbie (Stand-alone)

Kiss The Plug Goodnight (Stand-alone)

Throat Baby (Stand-alone)

Purple Reign (Stand-alone)

If you're wondering what this emoji means, ☐
Join the group for details. Click the link below.

Barbie Amor Book Trap

https://www.facebook.com/groups/1624522544463985/

Visit My Website
http://authorbarbiescott.com/?v=7516fd43adaa

Like My Page On Facebook

https://www.facebook.com/AuthorBarbieScott/?
modal=composer

Instagram:
https://www.instagram.com/authorbarbiescott/?hl=en

Made in the USA
Middletown, DE
18 November 2021

52799053R00119